Heartstrings

No Ordinary Family Book 3

LINDA BARRETT

DEDICATION

For Lizzy—

I'm very proud of the young lady you've become and for all your accomplishments, including your dedication to the oboe!

You are in my heart forever. From Grandma, the ex-bassoon player.

Cover art by Shelley Kay at Web Crafters

E-book and print formatting by Web Crafters

www.webcraftersdesign.com

CHAPTER ONE

He couldn't believe his good luck. Dr. Scott Miller felt as giddy as a kid with a double scoop ice-cream cone as he entered Boston Symphony Hall on a Saturday night in mid-October. He'd gotten a last-minute invite from his friend, Andy Delaney, whose younger sister was the guest soloist that evening. His older sister couldn't make the concert—thus, the available seat at the sold-out event.

"I'm looking forward to this," he said to Andy. "When I saw her play at Tanglewood two years ago, she held that audience in the palm of her hand. Including me!"

"She does know how to use that bow," said Andy, grinning. "Surprises me all the time. I guess…to the family...to me, anyway, she's just Emily, my kid sister."

"Who happens to be a violin virtuoso." Scott shook his head. "I play the oboe in the Doctors' Orchestra here in town. The group is great—almost professional—and we raise a lot of money for charity. But your sister's in a class by herself."

"Emily doesn't practice medicine and do surgery on the side," said Andy. "Cut yourself some slack! Geez, why do I hang out with such overachievers?"

Scott laughed heartily at his friend's remark. A power hitter for the Red Sox, Andy and the baseball team could all be called overachievers, training and training —sometimes overdoing it, too. They were all part of Scott's orthopedic practice at Mass General, where he was part of a sports medical team that included an array of therapists, trainers, nutritionists, psychologists and physicians.

They found their seats in the front-orchestra section, and Scott couldn't rein in his high spirits.

"I had a pretty crappy week," he said, "but music is my reward for dealing with patients who don't listen! Who seem to think all I need to do is wave a magic wand for all their pain to disappear."

"Wouldn't that be great? A quick fix. So, what do you tell them?" asked Andy.

"I tell them I'm a physician, not a magician. And if they want to heal, they'd better listen closely and follow up." He sighed. "It's the same speech I give to you and the guys, but sometimes…" Sometimes, his heart broke—like when he worked with the elderly and their joint issues, such as crippling arthritis. For these wonderful seniors, he wished for that magic wand, but settled for therapeutics and microsurgery to ease their pain and improve their lives.

Scott opened the program notes just as the house lights started to dim. Leaning back in his seat, he exhaled and relaxed. It didn't matter what pieces were showcased. Tonight, he'd replace his patients and responsibilities with the joy of listening to wonderful music—and finally meeting Andy's sister.

Twenty minutes later, after a short orchestral piece, Scott kept his eyes locked on the petite brunette who walked across the stage with the violin in her hand. She wore a long, sleeveless blue dress—plain, but perfect on her—and low-heeled shoes. He noticed details. A good physician had to observe, had to ask questions, and listen to what was said and what remained unsaid. Those skills came to him naturally now.

The audience welcomed her warmly, this hometown girl from a family well-known in the city. She turned to the conductor, nodded and raised her violin, then waited for the opening notes from the orchestra. In a heartbeat, she joined and led them through the long first movement of the *Sibelius Violin Concerto*. She played with the emotional mix of foreboding and delicate sweetness the piece required, before continuing through the second and then the third movement, which ended with a happy, upbeat feeling.

The woman was amazing. Thirty minutes, nonstop. Never faltered through all three movements, almost dominating the orchestra. The wild applause, the bravos, including his own, echoed through the hall until she left the stage.

The house lights came on for intermission, but he remained seated, just absorbing the experience.

"That's strange," said Andy, his brow wrinkling. He looked at Scott, stood and headed toward the exit. "She always plays my mom's theme song after each performance. I think it's in her contracts."

Scott rose. "Keep walking," he said. "I remember that, too. *Amazing Grace.* She played it at Tanglewood. I'm right behind you."

3

He followed Andy out and around and through some hallways, pausing while he identified himself to ushers and security. Finally, they knocked on a dressing room door.

"Em, it's Andy and a friend. Are you decent?"

"Come on in."

She sat bent forward on a cushioned chair, cradling her left arm on her lap, her left hand limp, her eyes shiny when she looked up.

"Andy! So glad you're here. I'm in a lot of pain. I can't drive myself home."

Her brother walked closer to her and knelt to her eye level. "What happened? In there"—he pointed back to the concert hall area—"you played magnificently."

Scott could have kicked himself. Some doctor. He'd noticed nothing wrong when she was on stage. But now he noticed a lot and couldn't restrain himself from speaking. "I'm afraid what happened, Andy, is that your sister abused almost every part of her body that she needs for playing. It's not only her hand. I'll bet it's her neck and shoulder, too. She's in trouble."

Her chin lifted, her eyes snapping fire at him. "And who are you, besides Andy's friend, who thinks he knows it all?" Her sharp words couldn't hide the painful gasps Scott heard as she spoke.

Her brother stood and looked Scott square in the eye. "She may not want to hear it, but I do. First impression, Doc?"

"She's an unbelievable violinist with a will of iron. That's my first impression. As to the rest…" Here's where he'd be the bearer of bad news, but not yet…."I'd need to do an examination in the office."

He turned toward Emily. "How did you get through this performance? Cortisone shots?"

She stood, turning her head to face him, and winced. "They're not illegal."

4

"True enough." He extended his hand. "My name's Scott Miller. I'm with Mass General's Orthopedics Department. Andy can fill you in."

She looked at his hand but waited. "Orthopedics? Do you want to test my right hand? There's just a touch of discomfort there too." She extended her arm, and he took her hand in his, but didn't shake it. Instead, he gently pressed her palm and the inside of her wrist with his thumb. Saw her wince.

"And there's the answer to what happened to *Amazing Grace* this evening," he said.

"I'll play it later at home," said Emily, "It's once a day for me."

Shaking his head, he said, "No. No, you won't. You shouldn't. From what I can see, your entire body needs to rest. Try singing instead. There doesn't seem to be anything wrong with your voice."

He grinned, slapped Andy on the shoulder and stepped toward the door. "I'll find my own way home. "And you," he said to Emily, "take care of yourself. The risk of ignoring injury is very high." He turned to leave.

"We'll need another driver," said Andy. "Can you take Emily's car, Scott?"

"Of course," he replied, reversing steps. "Should have thought of it myself."

"It can stay overnight in the lot," said Emily. "I don't need you—umm—I don't want to put you out."

Or accept a favor. "You've already given me some beautiful music," he said. "I'm happy to help."

She seemed to hold her breath before making the effort to stand. Taking a step toward him, she tipped her head back to meet his eyes. "Do you really want to help, Dr. Miller?"

He braced himself for what was coming. She'd want a miracle.

"Then get me through the new year," she said. "A couple of months. I have concerts scheduled—luckily in the States—Florida, New York, Philly, the West Coast. Whatever the cost, it's more than worth it."

He glanced at her brother, who just shrugged and nodded his head. "She's in the middle of the music season, and if she breaks her contracts...?" Andy emitted a low whistle in an off key. "That would be tough on her finances and her reputation."

So now he had to convince Andy too?

"Let me put it this way," he said, eyeing them both. "The longer you ignore treating the symptoms *properly,* the higher the chances of ruining your career—*permanently.* So, Ms. Delaney—Emily—you decide the cost."

This was so not the way he'd envisioned the evening. He'd pictured them all going out for a late dinner or a drink or even coffee, and celebrating her performance. Having a good time. What a dreamer!

"What-what do you mean by *permanently?"* she asked, her voice quivering.

He glanced at Andy. "Tell her how many players are no longer on the starting roster due to injury. And I don't mean a broken arm. I mean due to repetitive motion injuries. Especially pitchers."

Andy's brow furrowed, and he sighed. "He's got a point, Em. Brian takes care of his arm like it's a baby. The Astros have a whole medical team, just like we do, and our happy-go-lucky brother actually follows instructions. After all," he said, grinning, "he's a married man now, with responsibilities."

That comment drew a quick return smile from the woman. But then she closed her eyes, as if gathering her thoughts or her courage—he couldn't decipher which. Slowly, her lids reopened, and she stared at him for thirty seconds, up and down, but mostly at his face.

"Are you the best orthopedist in Boston?" she asked quietly.

"Boston is filled with excellent physicians," he said, hoping to avoid hubris—or idiocy—by protesting too much. "I always advise new patients to get a second opinion. In your case, Emily," he continued, "I should probably be the second opinion. Feel free to search out whomever…"

"No!" interrupted Andy. He turned to his sister, "He's the one. I don't care if you don't like his direct approach, he's the one you want."

"Figures," she murmured. "So that's settled." She looked up at Scott. "And you should know I'm stronger than I look."

"Stubborn is what she means," said Andy.

A tiny smile began at the corners of her mouth. Sweet.

"Sing with me, Andrew," she said, her smile growing. "Let's sing it now—together. As always, for Mom and Dad." She glanced at Scott. "Grace and Robert." Slowly, her soprano voice filled the room, each beginning note as beautiful as the notes of her violin. *Amazing Grace, how sweet the sound…*

Her brother's tenor joined her in a duet with an ease that bespoke a lifetime of making music together. Without quite realizing how it happened, Scott found himself creating a trio. And it sounded remarkably good. Two choruses of the hymn, and Emily made a cutting motion with her arm.

"Maybe there's hope for you," she said to Scott, a quick smile appearing and then suddenly gone. "I'm praying that there's hope for me. Because without being able to make music and soar with my beautiful partner over there," she said, pointing at her violin case, "I have nothing."

##

She'd packed quite a punch with her last remark. Of course, she was wrong, but her dressing room after the concert wasn't the place to argue. Scott sat behind the wheel of Andy's car, following his friend to Emily's apartment in the Back Bay area of town. Great neighborhood for a young professional like her...or him. But he was happy with his spot closer to the hospital on Longfellow Place, where medical personnel almost filled the building.

He watched Andy pull into what was probably Emily's or a neighbor's reserved spot and double-parked, prepared to wait. But his friend surprised him.

"Go on in with her while I try to find a meter. You need to get to know her a little. And vice versa. I think she trusts you now, so keep going easy on the keys, if you know what I mean."

He understood exactly. A softer approach. He exited the car quickly, ready to put his and Emily's initial introduction to rights, and walked to her vehicle. The passenger door was still closed. He tapped on the window and opened the door. In the glow of the streetlight, he saw big, beautiful brown eyes fringed with thick long lashes peep up at him. Dark chocolate eyes.

"I know you're in pain," he said quietly, "so you tell me how to help."

To his complete astonishment, tears started to fall, which made his heart almost stop. "What? What did I say? Your brother's going to kill me!"

"Sorry, sorry," she replied, rubbing her wrist across her eyes. "It's just that it's so hard to hide this, and now I'm not alone."

His breath hitched. A powerful statement, both revealing and true, but even though he was with her now, she'd probably hate him later as they moved toward diagnosis and treatments.

He swung the door wider while she pivoted herself around so that her legs dangled outside the car. She wiggled closer to the edge, preparing to stand.

"Your back?"

"No. It's my neck and shoulder, and of course, my hands. I'm a mess."

He offered his arm, and she steadied herself as she stood. "Well, that's an achievement."

"It's amazing how you played the concert tonight," he said.

"That's how it works. I was in another world."

"No pain in that world?" he asked dubiously.

She was quiet for a moment, until she eventually said, "Think of it as an out-of-body experience. I know it sounds weird, but that's the way it works—for me. Or should I say, worked. Past tense, because now it's more intense."

"I'm sorry about that. I suppose eventually you can't outrun your fears and have to face them."

A quick glare. "Are you speaking from experience, Scott?"

The sweet lady had a sharp tongue. "I've learned from the experience of my patients. Everyone has fears. And I don't live in a bubble, either. But have I crossed the line again?" he asked, gazing ahead. "I still volunteer as the second opinion, regardless of your brother." He pointed down the street. "And here comes Andy."

Emily turned toward her brother. "Can you get my joyful noise out of the back seat? I'm not leaving her."

Andy grabbed the violin, and they entered Emily's building, a well-maintained Victorian brownstone, the type often found in the Back Bay area.

She led them to her first-floor apartment and managed to unlock the door. A small entryway led to a large living room, which seemed to serve as her personal practice studio. Sheet music, music stands, a sound system for listening, and an upright piano as well as a sofa and table filled the space.

But Scott's attention was on the woman as he took out his cell phone. "I'm checking my calendar for openings," he said, "to get you into the office. Are you sure about this?"

"The sooner, the better," she replied.

He stared at the week ahead, trying to manipulate appointments. If his schedule was any fuller, he'd have no time to sleep. "Morning surgeries are set in stone," he murmured, shaking his head. "But if…okay. Maybe." He looked at her. "The soonest I could see you for an initial workup is Tuesday at three. I have to be somewhere else at four—but very nearby. So if that works for you, I'll put you in. To save time, you can fill out all the paperwork I'll send you ahead of the appointment and present it at the reception desk."

"Anything works for me," she said. "If you have a card, please write the date and time down and put it on the table. Holding a pen is a bit painful." She extended her right hand. "My bowing hand. It's really not too bad, and it's not swollen. As you said, I'll rest it."

He took out his wallet and did as she asked, then entered her phone number and email address into his cell. "In case something changes."

"Oh, I'll be there." She looked toward her brother. "Thanks, Andy. I owe you one."

"Just answer some questions and you'll be out of my debt."

"Not now." She glanced at Scott. "My brothers have a tendency to be over-protective. Both of them."

"We love you, Em. And that's not going to change." Andy started pacing. "So why were you alone tonight? Where's Mrs. Merri? I thought she accompanied you on concert nights. Where's your manager? Why did you drive yourself?"

She stepped back. "Whoa! Slow down." Her foot tapped several times. "Mrs. Merri has a heavy cold, and I told her to stay home." She glanced at Scott. "Mrs. M. was my very first violin teacher, and before that, my third-grade music teacher. Without her…" she shook her head, then addressed Andy again.

"And Larry's gone from my life." Suddenly, her eyes blazed hot fire, something Scott hadn't seen before. "That two-faced thief. Two weeks ago, at dinner with the London concert manager, we talked about future concert dates and costs, including my fees. The London guy kept saying that I was expensive but worth every penny of my fifty-thousand-dollar contract."

Her voice trailed off, her brow creased, and those lovely eyes became shadowed. "I was confused. My contract was for thirty, a fair and standard amount. And that's how I caught on to how Larry was fleecing me." She glanced from one man to the other and said, "I was so upset that I made excuses and left the table. He was gone from the hotel the next morning. Ran off before I could confront him."

She paused and looked at Andy again. "I guess Jen didn't tell you?"

"Not really. Just said that she was researching something for you." He glanced at Scott. "Jen's my financial whiz sister, with Fidelity, but it's Lisa, the lawyer, who should be helping get a warrant for the man's arrest!"

Emily stood still and Scott heard her inhaled breath. "She is, bro. She is. I guess no one is exempt from the reality of business, not even a concert musician." She walked to the sofa, held her head perfectly straight as she lowered herself, and gestured for them to sit anywhere they wanted.

"To answer your last question," Emily continued, "I drove myself tonight because I'm stupid! I should have taken an Uber."

"Or called me!" said her brother.

She glanced at the violin. "My future with Joy is what's upsetting me most. She's on loan until the end of December—only two more months! Normally, I'd be able to renew the three-year arrangement, but if I can't play, I'll have to return her."

Her voice broke, and Scott hoped she wouldn't start crying again. She'd been fearless about playing, fearless in her anger at the manager, fearless about getting herself to Symphony Hall. But now, her fear was at a breaking point. That was what a blend of worry and love could do. He'd seen it often with his patients when they first came to see him. When they left with a plan of action for determining a diagnosis and possible treatments, they'd become calmer. Knowledge was power— trite but true.

"What do you mean, on loan?" asked Andrew, regaining Scott's attention.

"Your sister is playing on either a Stradivari, a Guarneri del Gesu, an Amati or another outstanding Italian prize going back to the early 1700's," Scott said. "None of us could afford her — not even a slugger for the Red Sox—at least, not yet."

"He's right," said Emily. "I call her Joy. She's a remarkable Strad, an amazing girl who's meant to be heard, and not purchased by a collector and placed behind glass. If I have to give her up…"

"Stop borrowing trouble," said Andy. "Six months from now, you'll be on stage again, and this-this" —he gestured widely—"crazy interlude of legal and medical messes will be in your rearview mirror."

"I'd drink to that, if I had some wine," said Emily. "Instead, I'll take two pain pills and call my sisters in the morning."

"What are you—" began Scott.

"Over the counter, Doc," Emily interrupted. "No worries. I'm desperate, but not stupid—except for driving tonight." She grinned up at him, and for the first time that evening, he felt they were communicating as two ordinary people—man and woman.

He acknowledged her grin with one of his own and saw her eyes widen.

"You should do that more often, Scott," she said softly.

"Right back at you, Ms. Emily Delaney."

She looked more than pretty when she blushed.

The thought blindsided him. Pulled him up short. He'd trained himself not to notice those things, to avoid women he might want to know better. In his life, relationships led to trouble. He'd almost flunked out of college because of one. Had it been love? Sex? Freedom? Probably a combination. Where would he be now if he hadn't come to his senses? He'd come so close to disappointing his folks, such hard-working people and so proud of him.

The breakup had been awkward. He'd wished her well and soothed her ego. Assured her she'd been competing with his scholarships, not another woman. But he'd been careful ever since. From college to medical school to residency to being on staff, to building his reputation in orthopedics and then sports medicine—there were always goals. Further involvement with women had no strings attached—a mutually understood condition—involving none of his co-workers. Fortunately, making music with the Doctors' Orchestra provided an emotional outlet.

He'd figured out what worked for him back then. And after all his effort, the devotion to his career wasn't going to change. He wondered, however, if there was now room in his life for a lovely woman with chocolatey brown eyes. Or if she'd turn his life upside down. He wondered if he wanted to find out.

CHAPTER TWO

Lying in bed the next morning, in the moments before full consciousness, before Emily tried to move even one finger—nothing hurt. She sighed and drifted off again. Maybe it was all a dream. Or a nightmare?

Nature wouldn't wait, however, and she sat up, or tried to. Instantly, her neck protested.

"Slowly, Em, slowly." She talked herself into an upright position and made her way to the bathroom. At least her legs worked.

Last night, however, she'd had to ask her brother to manipulate the combination lock to the safe before and after she placed her violin inside. No playing with Joy today. She'd promised the men; couldn't lie to them, not with Scott standing patiently at the door, waiting for her agreement before he left.

Good-looking guy, very observant blue eyes—maybe too observant—and too smart. Sort of like all her older siblings. She'd always thought she was the least clever of them all. Forgetting things, day-dreaming… Her oldest sister, Lisa, used to say if Emily's head weren't attached, she'd lose that too, and probably on the MTA—Boston's train system! But she'd never, ever lost her violin.

After glancing at the kitchen clock, she found her cell phone and texted both sisters, using the voice function:

Can you talk or are you too busy?

Lisa replied first.

Spoke with Andy. The kids and I will be at your place in an hour. We'll talk then. We're going to take out a warrant on your manager. It's the only possible way to recoup any money.

Jen's message came next.

I'll see you later. Everyone's coming here to watch today's game and Mike's commentary on it.

Emily spoke into the phone.

I'm staying home today.

Lisa, bring your key to my place…and maybe a sandwich or two…for later. I guess this is a real white collar crime.

My goodness, who would have thought it?
But I assume a warrant is the only way…huh?"

Lisa's response confirmed her suspicions.

Yes, the only way to recoup anything if he hasn't spent it or opened a Swiss bank account. See you soon.

Emily disconnected and sighed. Everything always happened at once. Was that a law of the universe? Physical pain, unstable career, financial theft…

She looked around her lovely apartment. Almost twenty-eight years old and no one special to share the burden with.

The thought hit like a freight train, and she froze in place. A busy career where she was always on the go left no room for a personal life. A meaningful one with someone special. Of course, her sisters were more than special. They certainly loved her, but…she needed them more than they needed her. Both so happily married with families of their own, the way it should be. Inhaling deeply, she stood and headed to her bedroom.

"If I had a lover," she mumbled, "at least he could help me get dressed!"

##

Her bathtub was half filled when she realized she might not be able to climb out safely afterwards, so she let it drain and ran a shower, allowing the hot water to run over her. It felt so good—especially the heat on her neck —she could have stayed there for the rest of the day.

She managed as best she could afterward, her right hand doing most of the work, and if her hair dripped, and her skin was damp…so be it. Lisa would fix her up—do something with her hair—sort of like when Emily was a little girl.

Emily had been only seven, the youngest of the Delaney kids, when a life-changing accident had taken their parents and left them alone, and newlyweds Lisa and Mike had become substitute parents for her. For her older twin brothers, too, but Brian and Andy had had each other for extra support. Jen had been sixteen, way too old to be Emily's companion. Now that Emily was an adult, she was able to appreciate the dynamics far better. Poor Lisa and Mike. They'd certainly had their hands full.

Suddenly she paused and said softly, "Dammit! They still had." Her sister was running to help Emily again right now. So not fair.

Why hadn't she taken better care of herself? She'd known about musician's risks for injuries, especially for string players. The repetitive motion issue coupled with poor posture affected everything—muscles, ligaments and bones. What had she been thinking? Why hadn't she paid more attention to her aches and pains when they'd first started? Did fame make her think she was invulnerable? So wrong, wrong, wrong.

The doorbell rang, and Emily's great relief was tinged with regret. Despite her worldly travels and performances, she was still too dependent on her family.

When the door swung open, Emily's apartment filled with women's voices, children's voices, delicious aromas—it was filled with life! She stared at her two sisters and Lisa's children, Bobby and Briana, and moved as quickly as she could toward them. Tried to embrace them all and emitted a small shriek.

"Oh-h…I forgot…. But it's so good to see you. Thanks, thanks. You guys look so good to me. Almost stunning." Lisa, at forty-four with her dark hair and violet eyes, could turn more than a few heads, including her husband's. And Jen's auburn coloring had always made her uniquely beautiful. Her husband, Doug, had fallen in love with her from Day One.

Lisa addressed Jen. "Stunning? I think our little sister's lost her mind." To the children, she said, "Careful kissing your aunt, and then please unpack the food in her kitchen."

"You're very good at organizing everyone, Lis." Emily stood in the middle of the living room, as if watching a play. She was the lone member of the audience, though, since both her sisters were front and center.

With the children gone, however, they converged on her, and she saw the concern and worry in their shadowed eyes, on their faces.

"Let's all sit down," said Jen, "and figure this out. We'll wait for you to get comfortable first. If you can. Oh, God, Em, I can almost feel your pain."

Lisa shook her head and kept murmuring, "Oh, wow! You look stiff."

"Just my neck, and a little in my shoulder. It'll heal. It's my hand I'm more concerned about." Emily sighed and chose to stand, leaning against the back of a club chair. She now wanted to console her sisters. "Everything will heal, so I'm not worried—too much. Andy's set me up with his pal, an oboe-playing orthopedist who's supposed to be the best. He came to the concert last night, and I met him afterwards."

"And…what did you think?"

"Doesn't pull any punches. Very sure of himself. But polite."

"No big deal," said Lisa. "Sounds like a typical surgeon with a God complex. We've been around them during all of Mike's NFL career. His ACL tears, the meniscus tears. He's torn just about everything. But this is what I've learned, and it's important, so listen up: I don't care about any surgeon's personality as long as he or she has hands of gold."

Silence pulsed until Jen chimed in. "So remember that. Ignore the bedside manner. It's nothing personal." She reached for her tote bag, pulled out a laptop and got it humming.

"But this is personal, Em," she said, tapping the keys of the computer. "We can't help you medically, but we can help clear up where you stand business-wise and legal-wise."

"In order to get an arrest warrant, we need proof of wrongdoing," said Lisa. "Where are the copies of the contracts Larry Gaines signed with the venues you played? And I need the ones he gave to you."

Her world was starting to spin. *Get a grip, Emily. Think!*

"Everything's in my desk. Four different contracts for four different venues, two versions of each—Larry's and mine with the difference in fees—including the one from London. I called three places while I was still in Europe, and I'm contacting other concert hall managers as well."

While Jen went to retrieve the contracts, Emily held her stomach. "I can't believe he did this. What if he's stealing from other clients, other musicians?"

"They'll discover it soon enough when we succeed," said Lisa. "You still need to sign an affidavit attesting to what he did. Then leave the rest to me."

She was happy to.

"Now let's talk savings and expenses," said Jen, returning to the living room. "And other possible income. Any chance you have disability insurance? That would help now."

"I'm not sure. Maybe in the beginning, but I don't remember making yearly payments. Maybe Larry was supposed to do that?"

She caught the glance flashing between her sisters. "Okay, Em. Check your files when you can and let us know," said Lisa. "What about other expenses?"

"I pay for all travel, hotel, and meals, not only for myself but for Mrs. Merri and Larry. And he also gets— got— fifteen percent of gross. Geez, do you think he took that fifteen percent on top of stealing the twenty thousand each time? What a creep!

"I also pay for insurance on Joy, and that's quite a bit. But that's what all solo artists do. We all pay out."

"Understood."

Emily watched Jen browse the accounts she managed for her. "Oh yes, and of course, Jen—I also have the normal expenses here — rent, car, utilities. It never ends."

"How much is in your checking account?" asked Jen.

Emily shrugged. "I have no idea. Wasn't my checkbook in the desk too?"

"For crying out loud, Emily," Jen said sharply, "you need a keeper."

"Or a manager she can trust," said Lisa.

Sobs lay buried deep down inside. "Stop yelling at me!"

Both sisters stared at her as she continued, "You don't understand. I'd play for free if it were the only way to keep making magic."

Lisa rose and stood next to her. Lisa, her substitute mother. "We know you would. We know that nothing is more important than your music. But you have to wise up, Emily. 'Free' doesn't pay your bills."

"At least she's not in debt," said Jennifer, scrolling up the screen. "And, thanks to me, she actually has some good savings. But my guess is, honey, that you've been run ragged to earn this."

Her sisters were always so strong, so fearless, while she felt overwhelmed. She gingerly lowered herself to the arm of the club chair—an easier place to rise from than the sofa.

"My math skills are good, too," Emily said. "I wasn't worried about being in debt. But I wasn't paying attention. And you're right about being run ragged." She stared at her hands. "Just look at me! And it's all my own fault."

Lisa stroked her arm. "To play the violin like you do, Em, is a gift. A wonderful gift that had to be nurtured. And you did. No one knows better than we do the hours and hours of practice you put in, until you reached a level not many do. We were so proud of you when you won the Menuhin International competition. And you were only twenty-one years old! But most important, we know how happy your music makes you."

"And you did nothing wrong," added Jen, "so don't berate yourself. There was no reason for you to distrust Larry Gaines. How could you possibly have known he'd skim off the top of your contracts and pocket the money? If you had actually earned the higher amount, maybe you'd have played fewer concerts. Maybe you would have avoided some of this injury."

"Maybe I should have played less and handled my own travel arrangements," said Emily. "Maybe Mrs. Merri and I…"

"Maybe, maybe, maybe. But I don't think so, honey," Lisa said. "Booking venues, negotiating payment and dates, not to mention the travel, would have been mentally distracting and cut into your practice time. Mrs. Merri is a musician, not a business manager, but I've always thought she was a perfect traveling companion for you. And she loves you, too, like an aunt does a niece. Look at how hard she fought for you way back when, convincing us to give you violin lessons. And look at you now."

"It's a wonder she didn't notice your pain," Jen said. "And I'm so very sorry about everything. You don't deserve to be treated like this—actually, no one does—especially from a manager you trusted."

A betrayal. A betrayal by someone she'd depended on. The information made her dizzy, and ire started to build, but it was more important to get to her financial bottom line.

"So, deducting for the expenses I paid on all the tours, and my expenses here in town with rental and utilities, you said the balance remaining in my accounts is still good, Jen?"

"Let's put it this way: you're solvent and doing okay, but you can't afford to buy yourself a violin anywhere near as good as Joy."

She jerked up straight, as if a puppeteer had pulled overhead strings. "Who said anything about replacing Joy? I've got to get better quickly so I don't have to give her back. Maybe I'll sell my car for some quick cash. What do I need it for, anyway? I hate to drive, and I can take the T."

"Just don't leave your violin on the train."

"If that's your go-to line, it's old! I never did."

"But oh, God…do you remember she fell asleep…?

They filled the next few minutes sharing funny memories and catching up with Briana and Bobby. For a little while, if she sat still, Emily forgot her problems.

When her phone rang, she almost ignored it, not wanting to interrupt the good time. Taking a quick peek at the readout, however, she connected.

"Hello, there, Doc. Is this the new way of making house calls?" she quipped.

"Very funny, but I've heard it before," replied Scott. "Are you resting, or could you not resist taking your violin out for just a few minutes, which, in my experience, turns into hours?"

She couldn't tell if he was joking or not. "Isn't there an expression about short-term pain for long-term gain that could be applied here? But for the record, Joy is where she's supposed to be."

"Excellent."

"My sisters advised me to ignore your direct bedside manner. I think that's an excellent idea as well."

His warm laughter made her smile, and if the situation were less serious, she'd really enjoy herself. "But there was a caveat."

"What was that?"

"I believe the expression was 'hands of gold.' If I need surgery, I'm trusting you to have those hands of gold."

Her sisters stared at her, silent as church mice. She could almost hear them holding a collective breath.

"I'm going to provide you with the best care I possibly can, Emily, as I do for all my patients." His voice had become cool, distant.

"And I appreciate that, but keep in mind that this patient earns her living with her hands."

"So do a computer operator, a carpenter and a hairdresser."

Talk about being taken down a peg or two. Still… "And how many hairdressers in their twenties have you treated?"

Silence for a moment. "Hmm…point taken."

"Good." Maybe he understood, but it wouldn't hurt to spell it out. "I'm fighting for my professional life, Scott, maintaining my reputation, my name, doing what I love. There's nothing else for me in the world. I make love with Mozart or Brahms every time I play. And what can compete with that?"

There was another moment of silence before he finally responded, "I've got a great answer for you, but for the sake of professionalism and our relationship, I'll say goodbye. I was just checking up. So, take care, and see you Tuesday."

She disconnected, shook her head. "No heart. Absolutely no heart. How the hell does he play in an orchestra?"

Her sisters were eyeing each other and laughing, not listening to her complaints at all.

"What? What?" she asked, totally confused.

Jen could barely catch her breath. "What can compete with making love to Mozart, who's been dead for a couple of hundred years?"

"You gave him his laugh for the day," said Lisa. "Didn't you hear what you said?"

But that's the way it truly was. How it felt when she was lost in that cloud of gorgeousness. Silly to explain, even to her sisters. Maybe she was weird. "Glad to provide you with a chuckle, ladies."

"He does have a heart, Emily. And maybe the orchestra's the safest place for his emotions," said Jen. "Physicians handle a lot of bad news, stress, a lot of patients who…you know…won't recover. So.." she said, shrugging, "out of the office and into a symphony."

Emily stared at her sister in awe. "Great theory, Jennifer. I'll let you know if you're correct after I figure him out myself. He's…ah…intriguing. And safe. Andy had nothing but praise for him last night."

"Safe?" asked Lisa. "Have you had bad…"

Emily stared hard at her sister. "Why do you think I like having Mrs. M with me everywhere I go? Sometimes fans—even classical fans—can overdo it. She's fearless. And, really," she said, looking down at herself, "I'm not exactly a six-foot powerhouse."

"Petite like Briana," said Lisa, "but both of you are very strong-minded. Smart. That's how we measure ourselves."

And with that, her sisters gathered their purses and gave her lots of instructions. "Mike's calling the game today," Lisa reminded her. "So if you're bored after we leave, tune in. At least you'll be able to see him."

"Maybe she wants to come with us," said Bobby, who turned back to Emily. "The Riders are playing. It's not the same without Dad actually on the field, but they're still our team. If you want to come with us, you can lean on me. Then you won't be alone here."

Before Emily could reply, Jen began singing. *"Lean on me..."*

She was joined by Lisa for the next line.

Emily contributed her soprano while Bobby tapped out a rhythm with his knuckles on the table. Briana hummed along right on key.

At the end, Emily absorbed the scene and sighed. "Gosh. We sounded good. Even great."

"Thank Mom and Dad for the genes," said Lisa. "We didn't do anything to earn it."

"But we do have fun," said Jen.

"Hold on a sec," said Emily. "I just realized it's been twenty years since the accident. I was seven. Now I'm twenty-seven."

Quiet descended as they absorbed her statement.

"Now, that is a sad note to go out on," said Lisa.

"Well, we can't let that happen," said Jen. "Bobby, can you play something on Aunt Emily's piano to march us out of here?"

The boy grinned, looked at Em for permission, and provided the upbeat sound of Scott Joplin's *The Entertainer.*

Her family left a deafening silence behind them, too much time for thinking and no distraction from her physical discomfort.

CHAPTER THREE

Her Tuesday appointment with Scott couldn't come fast enough. Besides thinking about her medical issues, Emily couldn't help wonder if he'd smile at her again. The engaging grin he'd bestowed on her Saturday night had transformed him.

She spent Monday in a meeting with Lisa and her notary, whom she'd brought with her, in order to sign an affidavit. The form was needed to present to a judge who, hopefully, would issue an arrest warrant for her manager.

Then she relaxed to a couple of Haydn's cello concertos and drew solace from Brahms's Fourth Symphony—a blanket of warmth and the equivalent to comfort food. She'd turned to more popular selections, too. *Bridge Over Troubled Water* did the trick. Last year, she'd installed a Bluetooth connection to her stereo system, which she controlled with Alexa. Perfect for a person who finally got comfortable on the couch!

Resting brought some relief, and moving her body seemed a bit easier. Maybe all she needed was a lot of rest! Going forward, she'd be more careful to take breaks when she practiced. In the meantime, she'd have to be patient, bear the pain and wait for her hands to return to normal.

Which is exactly what she told Scott the following day in his office.

She'd arrived early by Uber, too anxious about being late, too anxious about everything he'd find out after all his tests, too anxious about what he'd say.

When she was led into his exam room by an assistant, he joined her immediately and she had one of her answers. The smile was back. His eyes were warm with welcoming.

"I'd shake your hand," he said, "but I'm taking no chances on hurting you."

"I typed half your paperwork with my right hand," she began, "then sent the rest to Lisa to complete. I was afraid to overdo it." She looked at her hands—the palms, wrists, thumbs—and almost sighed. "You're having a good effect on me already. Now, I'm feeling better."

His brows rose, and he turned to his staff member. "Another miracle. In only two days. Imagine that." He closed the exam room door.

"I've taken the liberty of asking Nina to be your personal contact in my office. She's an excellent nurse, but just as important, she's a musician in the Doctors' Orchestra, too."

Nina grinned. "Music is truly an equalizer among medical un-equals."

"A doctor's orchestra," said Emily, "sounds interesting and unusual. What do you play, Nina?"

"I've been playing the violin since I was a kid, but then I had to choose between music and medicine. Too hard a choice. So, I compromised."

"Sounds like double work to me," joked Emily, wondering how much "orchestration" Scott had put into this visit.

"Nina's helped me with other musicians," said Scott, "as well as the athletes. In your case, she'll be super-discreet in protecting your privacy. Your family's well known here in town, Emily, and gossip can run through a hospital as quickly as an Apollo rocket through space."

She would have kissed him if the setting had been different. "That's so thoughtful. I really appreciate your consideration. Mike, Andy and my sisters don't need to be fielding questions from anyone."

"Right. I want you to feel comfortable here," said Scott. "We will do everything we can to protect your career, your privacy. Vagaries to the press, but only the truth to you."

"Perfect. You won't lie to me. In fact, Scott, you can't lie to me."

His smile reappeared. "So can we forget the bedside manner conversation?"

"I suppose so," she said. "Although you managed it very well today."

"Then chalk one up for me," he said. "Now, let's get on with it."

After a half hour of thorough examination of her hands, neck, jaw, shoulders and arms, and hearing Scott murmur medical terms to Nina and asking her to arrange a nerve conduction study and MRIs, Emily considered she had reason to be concerned. Especially when she looked into his eyes at the end.

"I wish I could make light of this, Emily, and say two days in bed is all you need," he began, "but I can't."

"All I want to know," she said, her stomach twitching as though home to a bunch of grasshoppers, "is if my career is over. Can we fix this?" She felt herself blinking hard, and knew her voice sounded hoarse.

She saw the sympathy in his eyes, and her tears fell. Nina handed her a box of tissues.

"It will be a struggle," said Scott. "Time and physical therapy will take care of your neck and shoulder—assuming you commit to the exercises."

"Of course," she said.

"It's that left hand," he said. "The injuries are pretty bad for an elite soloist, but one never knows the future. So as to your career, I won't say no, but I won't say yes. I just don't know at this point."

She clung to a thin promise of hope.

"Let's review first and then go forward," said Scott. "I'll leave your hands for last."

To Emily, her hands were first. "Really?"

"Really. From the top down, you've got tendinitis in your neck and right shoulder," Scott began, "which means your tendons are inflamed and irritated. And why? Because of overuse. Think of your positioning when you play. Violin under your chin and right arm bowing, which affects that shoulder."

So true. "But the OTC meds help ease it."

"Unfortunately, they're not a cure."

A magic word. "Then what is?"

He glanced at his nurse, then back at her. "Remember what I said the other night? I don't deal in miracles. There's no magic bullet."

She nodded slowly.

"But I do deal in individual recovery programs. If I didn't, the injured pros I take care of would never get back to playing. The Red Sox, the Riders, the high school teams.

"So we can fix this, Emily — the neck and shoulder—with your cooperation."

Nina chimed in. "He gets very good results, too, with almost everyone. But it takes time. It can be a very long road back."

Hope rose again. They both sounded more positive. "You mean physical therapy?"

"For starters," said Scott, gently taking her hands. "All musicians are vulnerable—string musicians definitely included—to pain from repetitive motion and overuse."

He held her left hand and raised it. "But here lies your most serious issue."

"I'm listening," she said slowly, "so just say it."

She saw him check her out. He waited until she met his gaze before he nodded. "Okay, then. I'm very certain you have carpal tunnel syndrome here, as well as another condition called De Quervain's tenosynovitis, which affects the side of your wrist and the thumb."

"That's why my left hand is so bad?" she said. "Double trouble in one place?"

He nodded. "See how the base of your thumb is swollen? I also suspect the beginning of carpal tunnel in the right hand too, but we can handle that with exercises. We'll reevaluate after I get the results of the tests I've ordered, keeping in mind that surgery will be part of the discussion."

He paused in his speech, probably giving her a chance to absorb it. The warmth of his hands on hers was comforting, however, after that batch of worrisome information he'd just shared.

"I-I guess I hit the jackpot, huh? Two hands for the price of one."

"You will get through this situation, Emily. I promise you that in time the pain will be gone."

"'Getting through' is not enough for a concert violinist. I need to be better than before." Her breath quivered when she sighed. "Where's that magic wand when you really need one?"

"Keep that sense of humor," Scott said. "It will come in handy."

##

At seven o'clock that evening, Emily found herself sitting in a high school music room, near the string section of the eighty-member Doctors' Orchestra. Nina, that high-energy, clever nurse who'd taken Emily for her MRIs after Scott left for his four o'clock appointment, had had the idea. That appointment turned out to be a woodwind section rehearsal before the full orchestra gathered to play.

"Your hands may not work, but your ears and brain still function," said Nina over a simple dinner in the hospital cafeteria. "Music is part of the prescription."

"Does Scott know about this crazy idea?"

"Actually, he gets the credit. But I'm all for it. Why should you stay home alone, in pain and brooding, when you can be with a whole medical crew that's on your side? C'mon. We're not that awful. You'll enjoy yourself."

At the time, Nina made a lot of sense. But as soon as Emily actually stepped into the music room, she was overcome with doubt. The familiar atmosphere, with eager musicians tuning their instruments, had her yearning for her violin.

"I didn't think you'd come," said Scott, walking swiftly toward her, a smile mixed with his surprised expression. He turned toward Nina. "You're a great saleswoman as well as nurse. Thanks."

She waved and disappeared into the string section.

"I'm here," Emily said, "but I don't know why, except to prolong the time until I go home and make a lot of phone calls. Business calls." She glanced at her hands. "Then I figured I could do it tomorrow. Bad news can wait a day."

"Think of this as musical therapy," Scott said. "We're on the same wavelength in that way. I've also been thinking," he continued slowly, "about you and Joy. I have a suggestion."

Emily stood straight, ignoring the twinge in her shoulder. She'd consider anything, outlandish or not, to keep her violin. "What?"

"Buy time for now. See if you can negotiate a one-year…or even six-month extension…on the contract." He spoke precisely and she heard true regret as he went on.

"Each patient is different, and I can't see the future. I don't know exactly what your outcome will be in terms of performing at your previous level. But six months would reveal a lot. You wouldn't be lying to those patrons."

She listened hard, and her breath escaped in one whoosh. "Oh, Scott. You're brilliant. Just brilliant. It's certainly worth a try. If we weren't here, I'd kiss you!"

He laughed, shook his head, and starting walking away. Then he turned back. "I'm going to introduce you to your new therapists tonight." He pointed his oboe at a fortyish blond with a cello. "That's Carol Shapiro and over there, in the viola section, is Gail Shapiro. They're married to brothers who are not medical people. They do something with computers."

"Half the world can say that," said Emily.

"And by the way, since you're not driving, I'll take you home later."

The conductor mounted his podium. Scott quickly took his place and played the A note to which the rest of the instruments tuned. Emily folded her coat and placed it behind her to provide some softness to lean on. Although she didn't expect this group to match the caliber of the Boston Symphony, she was prepared to enjoy the interlude as much as possible. She'd guessed correctly, but they were good! More than good. Chopin études, selections from John Williams's movie scores, the third movement of Brahms's Third Symphony—a mix of appealing pieces for any audience.

She found herself "playing" with an imaginary violin but stopped when the pain started. Her eyes stayed glued to the string section, however, and bargaining with God came easily. She didn't have to solo anymore. If she could just recover enough to play with an orchestra, even in the last chair of the violin section, she'd be satisfied. It would be enough.

Really, Emily?

The violins needed more vibrato for the music they played right then. She glanced at the conductor, who was gesturing for that improvement. He seemed to know his stuff, and now she realized that Scott was part of a fine ensemble. No wonder he didn't want to miss his practice. Interesting, how music and medicine seemed like a perfect partnership. And these musicians had all put in a full day of work before coming to rehearse. Impressive. Hopefully, her new therapists would pull her through.

Afterwards, as the medic-musicians packed up their instruments, she listened to their cheerful chit-chat about being rejuvenated after a long day, how their fatigue lifted when they played. They spoke about their plans for community outreach. Who was going to hospice this week? Who was going to the pediatric floor next week? That was a cross-conversation that caught her interest.

Finally, Scott brought the two therapists over to her. "They'll set you up for a series of appointments. And you'll be working as hard as you ever have on the violin. But you won't go overboard."

"Scott, I'm not ten years old. I get it." She smiled at the women. "Thank you for taking me on at the last minute. I very much appreciate it. And I loved the music you guys made. Put me in a much better mood."

The therapists beamed. "Bring her around every time, Scott," said Carol, the physical therapist. "Love the instant feedback!"

"That's our goal," said Gail. "Improving the state of mind."

"We're trying to wrap a cone of silence around this—around Emily," said Scott, "for as long as possible."

"Hmm. I'm guessing that won't last long," said the PT. "Although, it's not as bad as having a published injured list in the sports section of the paper." She glanced at Emily. "Your brother Andy's had a couple of good years. He learned to follow directions a while ago."

"Well, that's a surprise. I'll make sure it runs in the family."

Emily looked at Scott, then at the therapists. She took a deep breath. "After I make a few phone calls to those involved with my career, the big 'secret' will be out anyway. I realize recovery will take a while. I made it through tonight by keeping my head and neck still. And ignoring my shoulder."

"That's my department," said Gail. "We'll work on sitting correctly, standing correctly and getting from one position to another." She patted Emily on the arm. "You'll get there."

"So, no cone of silence?" asked Scott, with a comically disappointed expression. "And here I thought I was creating a little of the magic you wanted."

She saw the two ladies eye each other, then look from Scott to her. They were definitely getting the wrong idea.

"Uh…Scott's my brother's friend. He's just helping out."

"Right. Moving heaven and earth sure fits that description," said the OT with a laugh. "See you soon." And they left.

##

"Well, that was a bit awkward," said Emily.

Scott shrugged and reached for her coat. "Step closer. Let me help you."

She complied, but added, "Your assistance is short term. I'm usually very independent." She slid her arms into the garment he held.

"And where did that get you?" he asked, leading her outside into the night.

"Oh, Scott, wait a minute. Look up. Just look at that gorgeous moon. I'm so rarely outdoors and at leisure this late. It's a treat."

He glanced up, but decided he'd rather feast on a gorgeous Emily. *No contest there.* "Let's take our time, then," said Scott, setting a slow pace toward the garage where he kept his car.

"Take a deep breath," she said, putting action to words. "Autumn is definitely in the air. I just love being back home in New England at this time of the year."

Engaging, honest, revealing. Boston was home. Her family meant home. Interesting. Her globe-trotting could have easily meant she preferred that excitement.

"You've been everywhere during the last five years — I checked this morning. London. Paris, Rome, Berlin and Tokyo—just for starters. And some places several times, I'd guess. Nothing in those faraway places to tempt you?"

Her laugh warmed him. "The truth is that I've been in dressing rooms and concert halls in all those cities. I think the only time I actually got to play tourist was in Florence, Italy. I insisted on taking time to see Michelangelo's *David.* And I did."

Her voice had lowered, and he could tell she was miles away, lost in memories. "And?" he prompted.

"Magnificent. It filled me like a concerto does," she replied. "Deep inside, in my soul." She paused a moment, and he waited.

"As the story goes," she continued, "Michelangelo said that David was already there, just waiting. All he had to do was simply carve away the extra stone! And what remained was...*David."*

"Yeah, that's a good one," he said with a chuckle. "As if anyone could have done it."

She laughed along with him. "Oh, no. There's only one Michelangelo."

"There's only one Emily Grace Delaney." They'd reached his car and he opened the door for her, then waited while she safely got in. "All set?"

Her warm smile sent his pulses racing, but a yellow caution light blinked in the back of his mind. No more bantering with her, he decided. Keep it cool.

"I'm good, thanks."

When he got behind the wheel, she said, "There may be only one Emily Delaney, but right now, she has no idea of who she is or where she's going. Her life is on hold, and she has nothing to give. All that girl knows is that she's grateful for friends."

Artfully put, but a message just the same. He should have been grateful to her. She'd just made it easier for him to keep his distance and ignore those incipient feelings growing inside. The ones that had lit the caution light.

But he wasn't a sex-starved undergrad anymore. Emily was not only beautiful, but the most interesting, vibrant, and curious woman he'd met in a very long time. Even in her painful state, her sense of humor shone through. Dammit! He wanted to spend time with her! He wanted to know her better. He was thirty-two years old. Wasn't it time to change that yellow caution light to green?

"Put my name at the top of that friends' list."

CHAPTER FOUR

Emily couldn't postpone making her phone calls any longer. *The hardest first. Just get it over with,* she decided. She tapped in the number of the Stradivari Society in Chicago.

Her wonderful violin was on loan to her through the society. The violin's owners were music patrons, a wealthy couple who attended dozens of concerts each year. Without their support, she'd definitely be at a disadvantage and using an inferior instrument. Joy inspired her. She had a personality! With that violin, Emily flew on a voyage of discovery—new intonations, new ideas—almost every time she played.

The downside, of course, was depending on the generosity of strangers. Emily returned their kindness by playing several private recitals for the Robinsons and their friends each year. All arrangements for loans, however, went through the society.

She whispered a little prayer while waiting for someone to pick up the phone in Chicago. Scott's suggestion stayed in her mind. A six-month extension…was that too much to ask?

Finally, she heard the familiar voice of Ann Marie, the society's coordinator, whose happy hello turned to sympathy in moments. She promised to do her best when speaking with Emily's patrons. "They might want to speak with you personally as well, so be prepared for a phone call."

"Thanks for the heads-up. I think that's reasonable. Joy is worth any number of explanations."

"Joy? Who's Joy?"

Awkward, awkward. "Umm. I've sort of renamed her. She brings me such joy, so that's what I call her. But we can keep that between us, right?"

"Of course. You're a joy to watch, Emily, with the aptly-named violin."

She hung up slowly, hearing the woman's chuckles over the phone, and wondering where she'd find joy if she couldn't play anymore. Wondering how she'd make a life without music.

Mrs. Merri came next.

"I blame myself," Jill said, still sounding nasal and hoarse. "I should have corrected your posture, insisted on shorter practice times. I wanted to…but you were always so focused, so into your playing zone…with all those concert dates. Maybe too many. But I was afraid to rock the boat. I truly regret that now. I should have intervened…I'm sorry, Emily. So sorry."

Tears threatened. "Not your fault, Mrs. M. Only mine. But I don't know when or if I'm ever touring again, so maybe it's a good time for you to build up your student roster." After assuring herself that her teacher had received total payment for the last tour, Emily hung up, exhausted. And angry again—at herself.

How could Mrs. Merri have been *afraid* to stop her? In the old days, Mrs. M had been fearless, fighting for and protecting Emily. The lessons, the Perlman music camp, going face-to-face with Mike and Lisa, insisting that Emily be given the chance.

She'd think about Mrs. Merri later. Now, she retrieved her performance calendar and prepared to make other tough calls. Cancellations. Those concerts she'd looked forward to in the States. There were so many! A dozen in November, nine in December. Two or three weekend dates with an orchestra was common, so more people in the area had a chance to attend.

This was the type of work her manager should have taken care of. Bookings and cancellations. And— the travel arrangements. She'd almost forgotten about that. Taking a deep breath, she began to unravel the next few months of her life.

Two days later, Emily entered the Outpatient Rehab Center which was separate from the hospital, to meet with Gail Shapiro. Occupational therapy. Standing, sitting, and evaluating her neck, shoulder and use of fingers and hands.

"You're definitely not the typical patient who needs total rehab in ADL — activities of daily living," said Gail. "But you do need some suggestions."

By the time Emily left, she had a dozen ideas to get through the day safely and with less pain. Some so simple, she wondered why she hadn't thought of them herself, such as wrapping her toothbrush handle in a washcloth to make it bigger and less painful to grasp.

Her friendly visit was like catching up with a girlfriend, even when she had to demonstrate how she'd move her whole body when checking for oncoming traffic—until her neck was free of pain.

"For you, this was almost a walk in the park," said Gail, after applying heat and massaging Emily's neck and shoulder "Wait 'til you visit Carol. She'll have you sweating."

"I'm sure you're right. The pain in my left hand is bad. Ibuprofen takes the edge off it, though."

"It does, but you can't live the rest of your life on analgesics."

Emily reached for her jacket and winced. "I would, but it's not doing the trick that I need." She said goodbye and left the building, wondering when she'd hear from Scott. Whatever the true diagnosis, she needed a plan and needed it now!

When her phone rang that evening, she'd expected it to be from Chicago. She'd gotten no call-back from the Strad Society yet and was on edge waiting for a response.

But the readout said Mass General. Maybe about her therapy with Carol.

"Hi, Emily. How are you feeling today?" Not Carol's voice. Definitely not.

"Scott." She didn't realize he'd be contacting her himself, unless… "Have you gotten the results from all the tests?"

"That's why I'm on the phone."

She heard the silence after his words.

"Uh-oh. I'm getting nervous. You'd better just spill it."

"Okay, then. As I thought, you definitely do have carpal tunnel syndrome in your left hand. It's pretty bad, which is why you're in so much pain. The good news is that's it's barely started in your right hand, which is why it hardly annoys you. You have options for recovery to consider."

Recovery. From horror to hope. "Okay. I'm listening."

"Do you have time tomorrow after your PT session? I'll have Carol start specific exercises for you. Then we can discuss your choices in my office."

"Sure. The whole point is to get better." She started to laugh and heard a note of hysteria mixed in. "I've now got lots of time, Scott. I cleared my calendar today, so I'm free. I called every venue where I was scheduled to appear and cancelled nineteen concerts. How's that for a day's work?"

Silence again. She could almost feel the gears shifting in his mind. "I'd say it was more difficult than any concerto you've ever mastered."

His kind voice almost brought her to tears. How did he know?

"Yes," she whispered, "it was incredibly difficult."

"I'd also say that you could use some company right now. I can be over in twenty minutes. How does pizza sound? And a glass of good wine? Or beer? Your call."

Did she want a visitor? She glanced at her familiar four walls, at the familiar furniture littered with music she could not play. So, why not? She trusted him. Besides, she was sick of her own depressed self.

"I can't promise to be good company, but if you're willing to chance it…? Sure. And wine, please. But do you really have the time?"

"Even doctors have to eat. Besides, I can't have Andy thinking I ignored you in your hour of need."

"Hour of need? Boy, I sound pathetic."

"You'll get through this, Emily. One way or the other."

"Right. Okay, then. See you soon."

##

By the time Scott rang her bell, she was starving. "You must have heard my stomach growl," she said after opening the door to a pair of sharp blue eyes that scanned her from top to bottom in one fast gaze.

His warm smile melted her defenses. "You know parking spots are at a premium here. Next time, I'll take the T and walk. Kitchen okay for this stuff?" He headed toward it without waiting for an answer.

"Sure," she muttered, following him. "Thanks for asking."

But the pizza smelled delicious, and the pinot noir looked tempting in her glass after he poured. She took a sip. "Ohh...nice, Scott. I like this a lot. And thanks so much for sharing dinner with me. The right prescription today."

He beamed as though he'd discovered the cure for poverty. "My pleasure, Emily. Nowhere I'd rather be."

She noted a sudden change in the way he was looking at her. Those blue eyes of his gleamed a warm light as he studied her now. Not as a doctor with a patient, but as a man with a woman. Instinctively, she returned his gaze with a smile. Nice guy. She liked him. Despite the bossy tendencies.

Her phone rang and she went back to the living room to grab it. Glancing at the cell, she shivered. Chicago. At this latish hour, she hadn't expected the call to come in. Then she remembered about the time difference. It was an hour earlier in Chicago.

Chicago. Where truth awaited.

She picked up the phone and returned to the kitchen while connecting with Ann Marie. The woman's voice was shaded with regret as she revealed her conversation with Emily's patrons.

"They wouldn't go for the six months?" Emily asked, in disbelief. "Why not? I'm not asking for a total renewal."

At the table, the pizza lay forgotten as Scott's attention was riveted on her.

She listened to Ann Marie in shocked amazement. "Three months? They said I'd know my future in three months? For God's sake, Mr. Robinson may be a doctor, but he's not *my* doctor! You can tell them I have the best in Boston.

"Oh, Ann Marie. I'm sorry to take this out on you, but this is the craziest negotiation I've ever participated in. We're talking about my life, my career, not a dollar amount on a contract."

She glanced up and saw Scott's concern all over his face. "You need six months," he whispered.

Nodding, she put the phone on speaker and waited for the coordinator to finish her explanation. Scott might have an idea afterwards.

"They feel that the Strad is meant to be seen and heard," Ann Marie said. "Sitting in a vault until next June is not good enough. I'm so sorry, Emily, that it's come to this."

"Can you hold on for a moment, Ann Marie? I need to think."

She stepped closer to Scott. "Any creative ideas?"

His steady gaze met her eyes. "Only the truth. With or without surgery, complete healing from carpal tunnel syndrome to the level of function you want will take months."

"If I ever get back there," she mused glumly.

"I can't make promises, Emily. But if it's at all possible, you'll do it. I have faith in you."

He did. She saw it in the warmth of his eyes, their serene, steady reflection of his feelings. She heard it in his confident tone. He'd be her coach all the way. But still...the decision was hers.

"Ann Marie? Thanks for waiting. Please tell the Robinsons that although it breaks my heart to lose Joy, I cannot accept the three-month offer. My job now is to heal. To play again, give concerts again. Adding the stress of an inappropriate and arbitrary date to return the Strad will make my recovery more difficult. Not good in the long run.

"So, tell them to find someone who will play that violin with as much love and joy as I did—let her be heard."

She hung up a minute later and collapsed onto a chair. Scott placed her wine glass in her hand and held his high.

"Not only beautiful and talented, but smart and classy. Honorable, too. In the end, you chose the high road, Emily, when you could have easily told them to go to hell. Cheers to you. Drink up!"

"Even if I did want to tell them to go to hell?"

"We'll raise our glasses twice for that."

##

They finished their meal quietly, each one engrossed in thought, but at ease with each other's company.

"Let me know when you're ready to hear the results of the tests," said Scott. "No rush. You've got a lot to process right now." And he wasn't going to put any pressure on her.

"Oh, I want to know everything, but in a few minutes. First, could you please unlock the safe and take the violin out?" She looked at her hands. "I can probably do it with my right hand, but I'd still have a hard time manipulating the lock.

"Sure. Lead the way."

They cleaned up the kitchen, and five minutes later were in her living/music room, the Strad's case open, the instrument gleaming in the lamplight, which showed off its beautiful red-amber hue. He watched Emily carefully remove it and hold it on her lap, on the sofa, stroking it almost as if it were a baby. He pulled a side chair closer and sat down, watching as she plucked a string.

"Out of tune already," she said.

"If you say so."

She grinned at him. "And to think you play a perfect A to tune the orchestra."

He enjoyed the teasing, glad to see she was fighting back, not allowing herself to grieve too much about her violin. "In time, you'll figure out what to do," he said. "You probably have insurance for your hands, so money won't be tight while you create a new game plan."

She cast a sharp look at him. "Will I need a new game plan, Scott?"

He leaned forward, took the violin and put it back in its case. He reached for her left hand. He couldn't postpone reality any longer, since she seemed to want to face it. A new game plan, she'd said.

"I don't know yet. But I can see, and you can, too," he began, "that there's swelling at the base and back of your thumb and side of your wrists. That's the De Quervain's. The sheath around the two tendons in your thumb is swollen, restricting the movement of those tendons. With me so far?"

"Yes. The tendons are being choked. Keep talking."

"Exactly." He turned her hand palm upward and very gently stroked the area near her wrist. "Remember the nerve conduction tests we did?" he asked. "It showed that your nerve impulses are slower than normal, which confirmed my own manual exam and diagnosis of carpal tunnel syndrome."

"Oh-h-h. Carpal tunnel for sure then," she said, her complexion turning pale. "It makes it so official when you say it like a pronouncement. So final."

"That's my job, Emily. I'd be a pretty lousy doctor if I didn't know a nerve from a tendon, huh?"

"I'm with you there, Doc!"

She was either unbelievably adaptable or putting up a brave front. "My primary goal, after the 'do no harm' imperative, is to diagnose correctly and help patients recover to their fullest extent. The nerve conduction test also revealed that you would be a good candidate for surgery."

She sat straighter and brightened up. "Then let's talk about that and about recovering."

He was going to throw a lot of information at her. A lot for a lay person to absorb. "Do you have paper and a pencil on that desk over there?" he asked, pointing to the paper-covered surface.

"Sure. Help yourself. Writing a book for me?"

"Nope. Drawing some pictures." He retrieved what he needed and returned to the sofa.

"For most patients with either or both of your conditions, conservative treatment is wearing a splint and doing physical therapy for four to six weeks or more. Months, in fact. If that doesn't help, we talk about surgery."

He began drawing a hand, palm down and thumb close to the viewer. "Here are the thumb bones, the tendons and this…" he said, drawing a darkened circle around the tendons, "is the sheath that we'd cut to release the pressure so the tendons can move smoothly."

"That's the De Que… whatever you said, right?"

"Bingo. As for the wrist—look here," he said, continuing to draw. "The pain in the carpal tunnel is caused by pressure on the median nerve. That's why it's inflamed and swollen. We'd have to cut the ligament pressing on the median nerve."

Emily remained quiet, and he did too, allowing her time to take it all in. "The problems seem similar to each other," she said.

"Yup. You're right."

"Caused by overuse," she said. "All my practicing over and over, the same motions. Hell, the same passages until they were as perfect as I could possibly get them. Perfect enough for Carnegie Hall."

She stopped speaking, and Scott waited, preferring to take his cues from her.

A brave smile showed itself. "How long is the recovery from surgery?" she finally asked.

"Anywhere from a couple of weeks to several weeks, but the area inside can be tender for several months. Patience is needed."

Those big brown eyes would kill him. "Will I play again?"

"You'll play, but I don't know at what level. And I can definitely say that if you return to all your bad habits, you'll wind up in the exact same condition next year. I'm serious about that."

"I am a total mess, aren't I?" she asked, her smile beginning to fade.

"A mess that can be cleaned up," he replied firmly. "Remember what Andy said about this situation being in your rearview mirror six months from now? Hold on to that thought. Free advice from a brother that's confirmed by your doc can't be all bad. At least you'll know your road forward in six months."

He gently took her hands in his. "You're not alone, Emily. You've got a big team behind you—medical and family."

"I know, and I'm grateful." She turned toward the windowsill. "Alexa, play Bach's solo sonatas." Almost instantly, her apartment sang with a violin's voice. "I will have to be the audience now." Her eyes closed as the music continued. "But I can play the music in my mind. I've memorized every piece I've mastered."

The woman was amazing. From his initial fear that she'd have a meltdown or two due to this change in her life, she was already figuring out how to adjust. He had confidence she'd also figure out her future on a grander scale.

"Would you like to come back to our rehearsal next Tuesday?" he asked. "Did you enjoy it enough? Or was it too amateurish?"

Her eyes snapped open and shone. "I'd love to go again, Scott. Thank you for asking." A grin appeared. "I'm not sure what you are since you're not being paid, but the Doctors' Orchestra is definitely not an amateur group."

He had to chuckle at her observation. "When I let everyone know your opinion, they'll be thrilled," he said. "It's a question we ask ourselves, too. So, thank you! And by the way, we're a non-profit organization. Our big concerts raise money for charities in the Boston area."

She nodded vigorously. "I figured you had a community commitment when I overheard plans for visiting a hospice and other places. That's such a great thing to do. In my student days, I played in nursing homes, community centers, wherever a need existed that I could fill. The audiences loved it. Good memories."

Her gaze rested on her violin, and a devilish little smile appeared. She peeped up at him. "'Seen and heard,' my patrons said. The violin should be seen and heard. How about I bring Joy with me on Tuesday and give your first violinist the thrill of a lifetime?"

He lifted his arm for a gentle high five. "She'll faint. That's a fabulous and generous idea—with a little zinger thrown in for the Chicago crowd."

"Exactly." She nodded strongly in agreement. "Glad you understand."

"A little payback is easy to understand." Good for her! He thought, and then went on. "It's the other stuff I come across that's hard to understand and tough to forget."

She cocked her head in inquiry. "I'm a very good listener," she said quietly, patting his arm. "Tell me."

He could believe she was a good listener. For both a musician and a doctor, listening skills had to be developed into an art. The words, the tone, the body language, too. Right now, everything about Emily's tone and body language told him she was sincere. He especially loved her touch on his arm. Nice and warm.

"I can't forget the anguish of every ball player who bottoms out. Think how Andy or Brian would feel."

Her eyes widened, if that were possible.

"I can't forget the anguish, and yet, the fortitude of every patient whose pain has diminished their quality of life." He took a breath, knowing he was about to reveal personal information he usually kept private. "My own mother is a hero to me. She's only fifty-seven years old and needs to use a walker. Has needed it for several years now."

"Oh, Scott. I'm so sorry. That must be just awful not only for her, of course, but for you, too—the one person expected to fix her."

She'd nailed it. Instantly understood. "I can help reduce the pain, but I can't *fix* rheumatoid arthritis." The words flowed. "No pretty shoes in her closet, certainly no high-heeled sandals...and no complaints." When he saw her compassion, he stroked her cheek. "You really are a good listener.

"I've had a lot of practice," she said quietly. "Like you."

Nice that she recognized that, too.

"Want to hear some good news?" he asked and galloped on without waiting for her reply. "I have a young patient—in her teens—with scoliosis. My team and I trained to perform a recently developed surgery where each affected vertebra is treated separately. We put in a screw and attached a flexible tether to it and pulled. She can continue to grow normally while the curve is corrected. Her shoulders are now level, her back is flexible. It is a so much better approach than inserting rods or fusing disks."

A comfortable silence settled over them before Emily spoke. "So miracles *are* happening all the time, and every patient is looking for those miracles that you can't promise. Even me, if we're being honest."

"Right. I can promise to do my very best. But that's all."

"I think, Scott, you should have thought twice about choosing medicine."

"Now that came out of left field," he protested. "I love what I do. When I think about that teenager…"

"I'm happy for her too. You can put money on it. But for every success like that…how many patients go home and just cope, even after you've done your best? It has to get you down sometimes."

She leaned forward, closer to him. "I've had down moments when the touring overwhelmed me, and I wondered what I was doing and for what reason. But when I thought about the music I've been privileged to perform…everything was okay again."

"I will do my very best to get you back to that skill level, but…"

"You're not God. My sisters were so wrong. You don't even have a God complex!"

He leaned back on the sofa and laughed the kind of laugh that reached deep down to the toes. So freeing, so lighthearted. Then Emily joined in. Their eyes met, and the laughing started again.

"That felt so good," she finally said when they could control themselves."

"It's what I would call a perfect duet!" he said.

"Exactly."

LINDA BARRETT

CHAPTER FIVE

Emily's hour of physical therapy the next afternoon challenged her. Carol demonstrated four tendon-gliding exercises to relieve the carpal tunnel syndrome in each hand, and gave Emily an illustrated printout of them. Emily quickly memorized the movements of every exercise to give her the freedom to do them anywhere and at any time. Then, the therapist worked on her neck with massage and stretching, which felt both good and bad. A full hour of work! Afterwards, she made her way to Scott's office.

He presented her with a Velcro-adjustable brace for each hand. Light and breathable, they protected her palms, wrists and thumbs—everywhere her hands were affected. Nina showed her how to adjust the pressure. They weren't too bad, but Scott's serious tone when he'd said, "twenty-four seven on the left hand, kiddo," made her think she'd be tired of them rather quickly.

Fortunately, her right hand was captive only at night, unless she felt she needed the brace during the day.

Some swelling had gone down due to her inactivity. A week of playing violin had been lost, but progress made, too. Good to know, both mentally and physically. Now, if only her neck and shoulder improved... She smiled ruefully when she realized she sounded to herself like an old lady!

A bell overhead dinged, and Nina left the exam room, keeping the door open.

"I'm on call this weekend, Emily," said Scott, "or I'd suggest dinner tonight. I never know when the phone might ring, and I'd have to run back to the hospital."

She held up her newly wrapped hands. "I don't think I can be seen in public anyway. But thanks." An unwanted thought crossed her mind. "Umm... Scott?"

"A question? Shoot."

She focused on his face, which, in his physician mode, usually gave nothing away. Her question, however, was personal, and she hoped to be able to read his expression.

"You've gone above and beyond for me a number of times now, which I think is unusual behavior, not typical for all your patients. So I want to apologize for misjudging you in the beginning. On the other hand, if my brother is pushing you to babysit me...he's in *big* trouble."

The man waggled his finger at her. He sported a grin and shook his head. "Your imagination is running overtime. Andy did not!" He took a half-step closer to her. "I enjoy spending time with you. I'd like to spend more time with you, see you often." His blue eyes darkened, all amusement disappearing.

"Oh..." That was all she could manage as his meaning registered. Heat flowed to her face, and she hoped she didn't reveal her embarrassment with a blush.

She didn't have relationships. She didn't have time. But was that still true?

"But you're not Mozart, who's usually my guy," she said.

"Nope," he replied. "And you're not the New England Journal of Medicine, one of my steadies."

The reading time he felt he required to keep up with medicine would be similar to her practice time. "I get it," she said with a nod. "And I will see you again on Tuesday—with Joy."

A twinkled appeared. "I appreciate the double meaning. I'll plan to drive you home afterwards."

"Yes. Yes, you can."

When her phone rang later that evening, she automatically thought of Scott. But it was Jen, who, after checking up on Emily's well-being, wasted no time with sugarcoating her message.

"The family is on a mission, Em. And that mission is you. We are not going to allow you to sit in your apartment for six months, waiting, wondering and feeling sorry for yourself."

"I'm not—"

"So, for starters, I'm going to pick you up tomorrow morning and take you to my rehearsal with the All-City Chorus. We're preparing a winter concert for mid-December. I'm not taking no for an answer."

"I'd love to go."

Silence. "You would?"

"Yes."

"Goodness, that was so easy. I was expecting a million excuses, a stubborn fight."

They all still thought of her as needy, weak or in another world. "I'm not a baby anymore, Jen. And I'm starting to think that these amateur musical groups aren't so amateur. They're worth a listen."

"You're making me cry. I'm really proud of you, Em. Wait 'til I let Lisa and Mike know. They're worried about you, too."

"Then I'll have to straighten them out."

"Which you can do tomorrow. The whole family's having potluck on Beacon Street."

Beacon Street—the house that Lisa and Mike had bought after renting for two years in Charlestown, and where a nine-year-old Emily had spent the rest of her childhood. "That sounds good. I haven't visited yet since I've been back."

"Well, you basically just returned—that concert of yours was only a week ago."

Only one week? And so much had happened. So many changes, her head could spin. "Hard to believe, Jen."

"Anyway, I'll pick you up at 9:30 in the morning and we'll go to the Commonwealth Theater. Is that enough time for you to get ready?"

"It's enough time. Please, Jen, let's make a deal. If I need help, I'll call. Just like I did regarding the contracts. So, just treat me normally, okay? Like any other member of the family."

She didn't expect the laughter. Jen actually whooped over the phone until she could control herself.

"Normal? Who's normal in this family? My husband runs back and forth to New York to help stage his Broadway plays and continues to teach at BU. Mike still runs after a football with his new broadcasting career, while your brothers, Emily, whether you ever think about it or not, are both key players for their teams in Major League baseball. And you travel the world, playing a violin so beautifully, it makes me weep.

"So, I ask you…what's normal about this family?"

Without a second thought, she had the answer. "Love, Jennifer. Despite your description, it's the love that holds us together. That makes our parents happy and proud of us."

"Oh, Em...." breathed Jen, with a sob in her voice.

Her fearless sister, who could cut through any problem, had the same soft spot they all did.

"Love you, Jenny. See you in the morning at nine-thirty!"

It wasn't that Emily was late, it was that she was only half-dressed. She tapped Jen's car window and motioned her to get out.

"When I need help, I said I'd ask. Can you button my pants, so I don't embarrass myself at the theater?"

Jen chuckled and instantly provided the service. "But Em, you're so thin. For cryin' out loud, you might lose the pants anyway."

"Let's get in. It's cold today." And it was. The end of October in New England provided a warning: winter was coming.

"Are my gorgeous nieces ready for Halloween tomorrow night?"

"Store-bought costumes that fit over their parkas. I didn't have time to be creative this year. And they keep growing!"

Emily giggled. "Children have a way of doing that, I'm told."

"Though you took your time about it, as I recall," Jen shot back. "Which brings me back to 'you're too thin.'"

With her splinted arm, Emily waved the concern away. "I'll gain weight now. I always lose when I'm on a tour. I never eat before a performance, so I mostly miss dinner while traveling. And I usually sleep in the morning after a concert. So scratch breakfast. And if we need to catch a plane, forget it. I can't eat."

"Neither of our brothers has that problem," said Jen.

Emily started to laugh.

"No, I'm serious. They're burning up calories like crazy, but they eat! They stay in great shape. You should talk with them. Maybe they have a secret. Maybe they follow a planned diet. Maybe you need a nutritionist."

"And maybe you need to slow down and stop worrying. Isn't that the theater?"

Jen pulled into the parking garage. "Plenty of spots on a Saturday morning. What a pleasure. By the way, besides some seasonal numbers, the theme for this concert is the Music of Broadway. I think you'll enjoy it."

"I always enjoy seeing you on stage, singing. You always look so happy."

"I am happy, hon. So happy that sometimes I'm afraid it will be snatched away."

Emily understood exactly what she meant. In a split second, they'd gone from a happy family of seven to five kids without parents. The breathless change could still reverberate after twenty years.

"Doug is wonderful," Jen continued, "and the twins are a riot and keep me laughing most of the time. I still love my job, and…singing is also a big part of the picture." Having found a parking spot, she shut the ignition and looked hard at Emily.

"I'm hoping that you'll find the same kind of happiness I have. I think about you all the time, Em, even send up a prayer sometimes. Maybe this forced rest will give you a chance to think about things, maybe reevaluate."

She would make no promises. If by some miracle, her hands were perfectly healed right this minute, she'd be back on tour with Joy. No question.

"Thanks for worrying about me, sis. Right now, I'm taking it one day at a time." She looked at her wrapped hand. "But I can promise you this: I do not want to sit in my apartment doing nothing. So today, I'm with you and looking forward to your rehearsal. On Tuesday, I'm going back to another rehearsal of the Doctors' Orchestra, where Scott plays oboe."

"Scott, huh? Sounds promising."

"MYOB, Jen. There's a line here."

Jen opened her door and walked around to get Emily. "C'mon. You've given me food for thought. And I like your attitude. Adults need boundaries, even with sisters."

They walked through connecting doors leading to the street near the theater's entrance and followed a group of people into the lobby.

In moments, Jen was introducing her to the other members of the chorus, simply saying that Emily wanted to enjoy her morning with them.

"She probably wants to check me out," said Jen, sotto voce, "to see if I still have it."

They laughed and told Emily not to be concerned. Emily smiled at the upbeat group. She could see why Jen had never quit the chorus, even though it took time away from her family. She guessed even career-oriented, married women with children needed something creative of their own. Good thing Jen's husband, Doug, understood. Maybe he enjoyed his time alone with their girls on Saturday mornings. Perhaps he relished it. Emily would ask him that evening. Whatever their secret, it all seemed to work out.

After Jen introduced her to their conductor, Emily took a seat in the middle of the tenth row—close enough to see and hear what should hopefully have been be a balanced sound. As for musical accompaniment, she saw a piano and a small chamber group of instruments — violin, flute, cello. About ten in all. It could work, since the focus was on song.

As expected, Emily heard a mix of Broadway and holiday songs—with complicated arrangements—throughout the first half, the director catching and correcting errors, trying to get the most from each vocal section. A serious and solid rehearsal.

For the second time that week, Emily admired how amateurs brought professional attitudes with them when making music. For the most part, they succeeded beautifully. Boston offered loads of opportunity for serious hobbyists. They were lucky to live here.

She hadn't expected a solo from Jen. Her rendition of *Don't Cry for Me, Argentina* had Emily almost in tears. Her sister still had a real voice and wasn't afraid to use it. She tried to applaud, and emitted a soft, sharp cry. Stupid, stupid, forgetting about her hands. Forgetting about…? But that was what music could do. Like a magic bullet, it could take you away for a while.

"Bravo," she called out instead. Jen waved and joined her as the group took a break.

"I seem to have earned the spot right before intermission," she said with a grin. "I think the director likes my voice."

"I certainly do," said the smiling man with a definite sprinkle of gray hair who joined them. "I need a favor, Jennifer."

Jen turned to Emily, her grin reviving itself. "Did you notice how he likes to beat around the bush?"

Emily chuckled and nodded. "Hello. I'm Jen's sister, who crashed your rehearsal today. Congrats on a great group."

The man beamed. "Thank you, thank you." But he immediately turned to Jen. "Linda McMahon is absent today, but I'd like to get a time check on her number. Could you sing it as though it were a real performance?"

"Hmm…*My Favorite Things* is for a true soprano. You know I'm mezzo. Why not ask one of the others?"

"I did ask two of them, but" —he shrugged—"they politely turned me down. They weren't sure they could do the song justice without rehearsing it. But I think they're totally focused on their own work and don't want to be distracted. Suggested I estimate instead."

"Oh, for crying out loud," said Jen. She glanced at Emily. "My sister will do it. She's got a beautiful soprano voice. And I can guarantee she knows the song. We sang it at home."

Home. In Woodhaven, MA. Emily had been little, younger than seven, singing with her mom, dad and siblings every night while they cleaned up the kitchen after dinner. She hadn't thought about those days in a very long time. Her memories were vague, yet here Jen was, speaking about it so naturally.

She nodded sharply at Jen. "Okay. I'll do it. For Mom and Dad."

Jen's eyes closed, then she blinked hard. "They'd love it."

"Do you have the sheet music?" Emily asked. "I might not remember it all."

The director beamed. "Of course, and thank you. Any sister of Jen's is a friend of mine." He retreated toward the stage, whistling.

"Look how happy you made him, Emily. He's got a lot of responsibility, but never seems to remember that there are always snags along the way."

"Glad to fix a snag."

A half-hour later, Emily found herself in front of a mic on stage, where Linda McMahon would have been.

She had the lyrics on a music stand in front of her, but after reviewing the song, didn't think she'd need them.

The familiarity of the stage wrapped around her like a comfortable shawl, along with a frisson of the unknown. Had she been holding her violin… it would have been perfect. She looked at the director and nodded for the music to begin, then sang about raindrops, roses, and kittens.

Perfect key, with an ease of delivery that surprised her. She smiled at the non-existent audience, she swayed and gestured when it felt right. And ended with a flourish.

She glanced at the director. A huge grin. Slowly she began to hear the applause of the other singers. It got louder and louder, followed by whistles and even a catcall. Whoa.

Turning around to them, she bowed. "Thank you very much. I'm not a real singer, but this was fun. You are doing a great job, and I look forward to attending the concert."

She took a step toward the stairs, then stopped and looked out at the theater. If she'd been playing her own concert…?

And for the first time in her professional career, she used her voice instead of her violin and suddenly began to sing.

Amazing Grace, how sweet the sound…

She felt Jen's presence, heard her beautiful harmony join in on the second line, and touched her hand, silently acknowledging a shared memory of their too-brief childhood. In the end, they actually closed the verse with the sweetest sound she could have imagined. It sounded totally professional, even to her own ears.

There was silence and then a smattering of applause in the rehearsal hall. But as Emily made her way down from the stage and back to the audience section, various choir members reached out to pat her shoulder or whisper their pleasure at her impromptu performance.

While the others continued their rehearsal, she found herself dozing in her seat. A big week behind her. Her hands in braces. Her future unknown. Whatever happened next, she decided, music would be part of it.

Scott's image came into her mind. He would have loved being present that morning. She pictured his blue eyes, alight with the prospect of having a good time—with her. Maybe she'd invite him to Jen's concert.

CHAPTER SIX

Lisa's house was packed with family that evening. When Emily walked through the front door with Andy, the noise volume hit new decibels. Four-year-old little girls definitely had high pitched voices.

"Auntie Emily, Auntie Emily!" They ran to her straight on, arms wide, and would have knocked her over had Andy not swooped them up.

"What am I?" he asked. "Chopped liver?"

Laura and Lily giggled. "Higher, higher!" He tossed one to their dad. "Here you go, my man. Higher, higher," he imitated.

Emily watched her nieces sail like birds with their arms waving aloft. She laughed along and felt like flying, too.

"Lisa! It's so good to be home." She hugged her oldest sister as though she hadn't seen her in years, when it had only been a week.

Lisa returned the embrace and said, "Your suite is still available upstairs if you want to lay low here for a while. You know, until your hands get better."

She didn't have to think twice. "Thanks a lot, Lis, but I'm okay. After I get some pants that just pull up, I won't even have a button problem."

"Got it all figured out, huh?"

"Working on it."

Shorthand speech between sisters. Emily understood that Lisa's questions covered a lot more territory than pants with elastic waistbands.

"Good," said Lisa, giving her a hug. "I like 'working on it.' Just remember, you're not alone."

Emily's glance covered the other nine gathered family members. "How can I forget?"

Only her brother, Brian, and his wife and stepson were missing. Since he played for the Houston Astros, that Texas city was his home now. Instant family. He adored his "Meggie" and Josh. The entire clan, including the four kids, had celebrated the wedding in Houston last winter—in between sports seasons.

She gave Andy a swift look. "I guess you and I are the only holdouts."

"About what?"

"Well, look at Jen, Lisa, Brian—all living the happily-ever-after life. We're the holdouts."

"Kiddo," began Andy, "you can hold out for your Mozart, but the only thing I'm holding out for is the right woman."

Laughing, she said, "Sounds like a plan. I wish you the best of luck."

"Back at you. How's Scott these days?" His green eyes gleamed with humor.

And damned if she didn't feel the heat rise to her face again. "On call this weekend."

"Interesting that you know these details." He chuckled and moved off, calling for Bobby.

Scott would have enjoyed himself tonight with her family. He would have fit right in, too. But would she have asked him to come? Probably not. Too personal. Too soon. Nope, she wasn't ready. With an unknown future, everything in her life was on hold. Including men. Maybe she should tell him that.

It hit her once more, as she absorbed the scenes before her, that she'd never have that happily-ever-after if she continued her solo career, playing all over the world. It worked fine for musical couples. They thrived. She could think of several, starting with the love story of Clara and Robert Schumann in the 1840s. She could think of many strong marriages between a male musician with a supportive wife, like her own dear Maestro Itzhak Perlman, whose wife knew music and played well but didn't perform. But between a traveling female soloist and a non-musician husband with a strong career of his own? Her mind went blank. Couldn't come up with even one example. Maybe because it just didn't work.

"Aunt Emily, you look sad. Come with me and I'll play for you. That always makes you happy."

Emily wrapped her arms around her precious niece, Briana. A petite brunette, so similar in looks to Emily, she could have been taken for her own daughter.

"You're so right, my love. Show me what you've learned since last time I was here."

Briana wrinkled her nose and led Emily upstairs to the bedroom floor. "Did you know Mom and Dad have just given me some new rules?"

"Like what?"

"I have to take a ten-minute break every hour even if I'm not tired. I have to listen to my body and take breaks when I *am* tired. I have to be careful of my posture as I sit in the chair. I have to do warm-up exercises for my hands before playing.

"There are a lot of new rules, now," she said glumly, "and all I want to do is play my viola."

She sat on Briana's bed and motioned the child to sit next to her. Apparently, her sister and Mike had wasted no time with their research and instituting those rules.

"Playing is the reward after the rules. It's the Boston cream pie after a plain old chicken dinner. Know what I mean?"

"Yes. If I skip the dinner, I'll get into trouble like you did." She looked at Emily with a compassion and understanding that went beyond a nine-year-old's grasp. And yet, she was only nine. Then she glanced at Emily's hands.

"Does it hurt you, Aunt Emily?"

"Not much. What really hurts is that I can't play my violin anymore, not for a long time."

The girl nodded her understanding. "I get it. I'd feel terrible if I had to stop playing." She moved a chair to the middle of the floor, set up her music stand and took out her viola. Then she sat down. "Straight back, exercise wrists." She demonstrated as she spoke.

"Perfect," encouraged Emily. "I'm proud of you, honey. It's very important."

Finally, Briana lifted the viola, took the bow, tuned the instrument, and began to play.

##

"You've got quite a musician here," said Emily an hour later, as she and Briana rejoined the family. "And she followed all the rules."

"I wish we'd known to set them down for you!" said Mike. "We're not making the same mistake twice in this family." He came closer and offered a protective hug. "You can bunk with us while you heal."

"Still looking out for me, huh?" she asked.

"Always."

"Funny how life goes. Just when I think I'm all grown up...bam! Stupidity." She held out her hands, one wrapped, one free.

"I disagree, honey. You made a mistake, and that can occur at any age. Stupidity only happens when you don't learn from the mistakes."

He'd been the best big brother-dad combination she could have asked for, and he was still on the job. He had Lisa and his own two children. At this point, Emily should have been an afterthought.

"I'm learning from my current fiascos, Mike, and figuring things out. You don't have to worry about me at all anymore."

He threw back is head and laughed. "It doesn't work like that, baby." He gestured around the entire room. "Your sister and I raised the lot of you. You're all part of us. Our concern doesn't end when you reach that legal twenty-one."

"I'm way beyond that," she said.

"Proving my point," he said, "but I hear that Scott's taking good medical care of you."

"You did?" She thought about the Doctors' Orchestra, and his swiftness in setting up her appointments. "I think he is." She nodded toward Andy. "Your source?"

"No secrets around here when it comes to the health and well-being of our family." He pivoted and wore what Emily called his "serious" expression. "I've known Scott Miller for a few years now. I retired before he had a chance to operate on what would have been my next injury. But he has a good reputation as a surgeon."

"That's what everyone's telling me," she said, as suspicion began to grow in her mind. "Andy vouched for him, too. So now I'm thinking you're all in cahoots and setting me up for a definite surgery. Has Scott said something to Andy? Because although I'm leaning that way, I haven't quite made up my mind yet."

"No! Absolutely not, Emily. That would almost be malpractice for him. You'd be the first to know. Doctor-patient privilege, remember?"

"Well, it wasn't like that with you. Everyone in Boston, heck, in the country, knew about every injury you got."

She heard her cell ring in the near distance and ran to get it while calling over her shoulder, "Be right back."

On a Saturday night, not many friends would be calling except…maybe…a bored physician? She glanced at the ID, smiled, hit speaker and looked for a quiet corner where she could retreat.

"Hi, Scott. How's the on-call going?"

"Did rounds this morning with the residents, went to the gym, then home and took three calls. When the fourth call came, I headed back in. I'm still at the hospital. But I needed a break."

Something in his voice caught her attention. "Was it an emergency?" she asked softly.

"I guess for the new parents, yes. Their baby son was born with a clubfoot."

"Oh…?"

"Do you know what that is?"

"Uh…I should have paid more attention in science class."

"It's where the foot is twisted out of normal position. It's actually pretty common, about one in a thousand births, but to these two new parents…their world had shattered."

"Oh, man," she said, staring at her nieces and wanting to hug them to her.

"And when I tried to refer them to a pediatric orthopedist," he said, "they insisted they wanted me. Why would they do that?"

"Because they liked your bedside manner?" Now she swallowed a giggle.

His warm laughter joined hers at their little inside joke. "But Em, you don't make important decisions based on 'like!'"

"Let's get creative for a minute. Can you tell them you've never worked with babies before?"

"That would be a lie. And I've handled clubfoot, too. But infants are not my specialty. I'll have to use a different approach when I see them tomorrow."

"So sorry, Dr. Miller. You would have had a better time at my sister's house tonight."

"No doubt. I know Mike fairly well, and Andy is a friend. But at this point, Ms. Delaney, the invitation has to come from you."

He sounded serious. Showing his cards, but she could tell he wasn't playing a game. Scott was different from her admirers who waited at the stage door after a performance, hoping for private time. She'd never considered it. She'd thanked them, smiled, waved, and walked to the car, already thinking about the next concert. But now, there were no concerts.

"Is that the way it works?" she asked. "We exchange invitations?"

She heard Lisa's happy voice in the next room; she heard Jen's reply. Was she heading toward a more family-oriented lifestyle now, too? And was Scott the one or only the first? Guess she'd have to find out. God, she was such an ignorant nerd.

"Let's say that right now, the ball is in your court," Scott said. "Not that I can picture you smashing one over the net."

"Well...certainly not with these hands," she said, at ease now instead of uptight. "But don't underestimate me. Just this morning, Scott, I'd decided to invite you to attend Jen's concert with me. It's in a month or so. How's that for a return volley over the net?"

"Absolutely perfect. I accept with pleasure. And if I'm on-call again, I'll change schedules with someone else."

Definitely showing his cards.

##

Emily took a cab to Scott's rehearsal on Tuesday night, with Joy securely tucked under her arm. She was looking forward to hearing Joy's voice again, released tonight by Dr. Anna Klein, cardiologist, and first chair violinist in the volunteer orchestra. Scott had filled her in, told her Anna was so eager, she'd probably show up early. So Emily planned to arrive early, too. She briefly wondered about her own reaction to seeing Joy handled by someone else. A factor that wouldn't have emerged had she just returned the violin to Chicago.

Sighing at herself for being a glutton for punishment, she entered the practice room and recognized Anna from the week before.

"Hello again, Emily," said the doctor, her eyes moving toward the cased instrument. "You really did bring your violin?"

"Of course," said Emily, "I wouldn't joke about such a thing." She put Joy on a nearby chair and tried to shrug her coat off. Anna immediately helped. "I know where you sat last week," the woman said, folding and placing the coat on the same chair.

She returned and looked at the treasure. "May I?"

"Absolutely," said Emily, swallowing hard. "She hasn't been played in ten days. You'll have to tune her..." Her voice trailed off as she watched Anna unlock the case and heard the woman exhale.

"She is beautiful just to look at."

The wood glowed, even while lying in a case. "Please, Anna, pick it up and play for me," said Emily. Her stomach had butterflies, her heart held sorrow, but she needed to begin her goodbyes.

A minute later, Anna finished tuning and began playing the melody of Smetana's *The Moldau* with the excellence and passion a first violinist was expected to possess. Images of a flowing river and the sweetness and sorrow of the piece entered Emily's soul. The symphonic poem paid a musical homage to the composer's homeland of what was now the Czech Republic.

Behind Emily were whispers. Shushes. Then Anna transitioned to *Hatikvah,* the Israeli national anthem where the *Moldau's* theme had resurfaced. The room was silent. Until the very end of the last note.

Then applause burst from Anna's peers—from musicians who appreciated the work. From Emily too, although her tears streamed so hard, they dropped to the floor. And then a pair of strong arms held her—and she leaned back.

Concern limned Scott's face when she finally looked up. "They were right," she gulped, wiping at her cheeks. "Joy is meant to be seen and heard. Look at their pleasure..." Her glance encompassed the crowd. "But I'm not the one...I'm not the one..."

Anna came over just then and tried to return the instrument.

"No, no," said Emily, shaking her head. "It's yours for now. I'll bring her every week for you until I have to ship her back." She managed to smile at the doctor. "This is a once-in-a-lifetime offer, Anna. You can't refuse. And we'll all enjoy the music you make, including me."

Anna threw a hard glance at Scott. "Are you handling her case?"

"I am. She hasn't decided to have the surgery yet. We'll see. But she knows that healing takes a lot of time. We're hoping for full recovery."

"Of course. We always hope." She patted Emily's shoulder. "Did you know that *Hatikvah* means the hope? A good coincidence."

Emily watched the rest of the ensemble find their places while she sat in her own chair. Anna meant well, but Emily's gut said otherwise. *Hope* didn't guarantee a complete recovery. And her left hand was really bad. Her instincts were kicking in, urging her along a different path for reasons she did not quite understand yet.

Her gaze traveled to Scott, and a warmth filled her. She felt the corners of her mouth curve up. She liked him. Liked him a lot. And not like a brother! A new experience.

As if Scott felt her eyes on him, he turned his head slightly, and bestowed a captivating smile before raising his oboe and providing the A note for his friends.

If he suggested going for coffee later on, she'd go. Despite the possibility of spilling it.

CHAPTER SEVEN

Emily ordered a hamburger and fries along with her coffee, and Scott did the same. "I honestly had no idea how hungry I was until my stomach started growling. Good choice of place." A clean, neat, late-night bistro with tantalizing aromas.

"Glad to oblige," said Scott, "but it doesn't take a genius to find food in this neighborhood. Between all the hospitals and affiliated buildings—the staffs and shifts— people wander in at different times. Most of the restaurants stay open late."

She leaned back in the booth. "That makes sense, but I bet it's mostly the single workers who grab food at night. Mike always wanted to get home as soon as possible after a training day or a game."

His glinting blue eyes should have warned her. "Are you saying, 'there's no place like home,' Dorothy?"

Enjoying this playful side of him, Emily relaxed and got ready to spar. "I'm certainly no example of home life," she said. "My apartment is convenient. But a home?" She pictured herself packing and unpacking, arriving and departing with mere days in between. "Uh-uh. You don't need to be a wizard to see it's just a stopping-off place for me now."

In the beginning, however, with fewer concert dates, she'd enjoyed choosing curtains and furniture. She'd enjoyed turning her living room into a practice studio with a piano for an accompanist when prepping for a recital. She really did miss that fun. And didn't like this question.

"What about you?" she challenged, leaning forward. "You live alone, too."

"Right," he said. "The difference between us is"— his voice deepened as he added suspense—"plants. I've got plants. All kinds — big floor plants, small plants for tables."

She didn't get it immediately. "Plants?"

"You know…those pretty green things that grow— if you nurture them." He shot her a wide grin, and her tension dissolved. "I'm a nosy guy, Emily. Are you ready for some flowering plants in your life, or is a stopping-off place all you want?"

What a way to phrase the choice! "It's not about *want,* Scott. That's how you grow a career. And I'd probably kill those plants anyway."

His eyes captured hers. "I don't believe that for a minute. You're a sensitive, caring person, and generous. Look at what you did for Anna, and how you wanted to coach the string section. I'm afraid, Emily, you've got no killer instinct at all!"

Totally amused now, she said, "I'm crying uncle! You've got me going in circles, Scott."

"Hm…that wasn't my intention," Scott said, "but maybe it's not a bad thing. Perhaps your focus might change now. Maybe greenery will tempt you. At least for a little while."

She sighed and nodded. "For perhaps longer than a while. I might redecorate and burrow in."

His brows lifted and he leaned toward her across the table, gently taking her hands in his, splint and Velcro, too. "Music is yours—for life. You will play again, Emily. We just don't know at what capacity."

She believed him, and for a hobbyist, his assessment would have been great. But for her? "Thanks for that encouragement. And for including me in your rehearsals. I enjoy them a lot, even though I sometimes want to jump up and take over."

"They won't mind suggestions coming from Emily Delaney."

Shaking her head, she said, "That's up to the conductor. So, when is your big concert? And please don't say it's the same date as Jen's, on Saturday, the eleventh."

The food arrived before he could answer. Emily gasped at the size of the burgers on their plates. Huge— piled high with tomato, lettuce, sliced pickle.

"Holy Toledo, Scott. I'm cutting this in half. Tomorrow's lunch might be here, too."

She managed to lift one half of the monster with her free hand and took a bite. "Mm… good." She needed to support it with her left hand, too. "Worth looking like a dork."

They both dug in and took the edge off their appetites.

"I hope you like it, Em, because I think tonight counts as our first date, and I don't want to disappoint you."

She glanced up quickly, saw the gleam in his eyes, and laughed with him. "Some date. I'm making a mess. The girl has no table manners!"

He waved his hand. "You're doing great. I can come up with more important criteria."

Well, that covered a lot of territory. She'd think about it later. "So how long have you played the oboe, Scott?"

His brow furrowed. "I want to say all my life, but I started in middle school. I already played the piano, the one in my friend's basement. So learning another instrument—one that I could take home—seemed like a good idea. To be honest, I didn't exactly choose the oboe. The school put me in a woodwinds class, and there it was. I actually play the clarinet as well." A slow smile crossed his face. "Happy to say that it all worked out, and now you know the entire musical history of Scott Miller."

"Are you kidding? I have a million questions," Emily said.

"Such as…?

"Who taught you the piano? How come you played at your friend's house? Did you ever take private lessons on the oboe? Or the clarinet?" She reached for his hand. "You really are very good, Scott. Your pitch is perfect. You'd be great in a woodwind quartet."

She loved the sound of his warm laugh. "Thanks, Emily. That's high praise. All I'd need is a forty-eight-hour day!" He took a sip of his coffee. "Regarding that piano at my friend's house… do you know the old story about the bank robber, Willie Sutton? And what he said when asked why he always hit up banks?"

"Nope."

"'Cause that's where the money is.'"

She chuckled along with Scott. "Makes a lot of sense."

"Well, it applies to me, too. The piano was in Ryan's basement, so that's where I went. His mom played pretty well, and she took time to show me around the keyboard."

As Emily watched, he seemed to drift off in memories. "It was a lot of fun."

"Did you play by ear?"

He nodded. "Mostly. Other kids were messing with guitars, but I didn't have one of those either. And considering I ran track in the fall, played baseball in the spring and worked part-time jobs as soon as I could, as well as going after high grades, I wouldn't have had the time."

She guessed his parents didn't have much money. "We sang."

"Excuse me?"

"Singing is what I remember," Emily said. "We sang every night after dinner. My mom and dad could both carry a tune really well, and my dad told silly jokes. And everyone cracked up, and my mom said, 'Oh, Robbie.' I don't remember a single joke, but the twins mimicked him and when we sang *Row, Row, Row Your Boat,* my dad changed the words, and we sang, 'Emily, Emily, Emily, Emily, life is but a dream.' I remember that. And I remember the feelings…you know what I mean?"

Her memories had poured out of her like a runaway train, and she was breathless now, choking back an unexpected sob. She glanced at Scott and then looked away, but his hands wrapped around hers.

"Yeah. Yeah, I do know what you mean," said Scott. "It was the same with us—my folks, my brother and sister and me. Not the singing, but the family feeling, the love. My sibs remained outside of Pittsburg where we grew up. I knew I wanted medicine early on and would have gone to any school that accepted me—and offered some scholarships."

And suddenly, he wasn't the big-shot surgeon in a prestigious hospital giving orders to everyone around him. He was simply a man, who'd once been a boy with dreams. And who'd worked hard to achieve them.

"I'm glad your scholarships brought you to Boston, Scott, and I'm glad Andy brought you to my concert."

"I'm glad, too. But let's be honest here…you weren't so happy at the time."

She waved her hand in dismissal. "Oh, please. It's a woman's prerogative to change her mind."

He laughed hard, and she didn't get it. "What?" she asked. "What did I say?"

But he asked for the check, and a minute later they were back in his car, heading toward her house.

##

A woman's prerogative? Scott sat behind the wheel, swallowing more laughter, not wanting to insult her nor wanting to dismiss her. If it weren't for her accomplishments as well as her actual age, she could fool people into believing she was a college girl instead of a career woman.

Except—she moved like a woman, worked like a mature woman with a plan, and tried to handle her tough medical issues. Life hadn't handed her a bowl of cherries. Same for her siblings. He'd say all five Delaneys had been tried by fire. And survived. He admired that.

"Did Andy tell you he's going down to his place in Florida for a while?" asked Scott with a bit of caution.

"Yes, he told everyone at my sister's house Saturday night. He'll go to Brian's for Thanksgiving in Houston and be back here for Christmas."

"I bet Brian's happy about that," said Scott.

"So's Josh, his stepson. Now the kid can show off two Major League players to his friends." Her gentle laugh was infectious, and he found himself joining in.

"I wonder why Andrew bought a place in Florida," she continued to muse. "Except for Brian, we're all up here."

"C'mon, Em. He's a single guy," said Scott. "And his off-season lasts for several months. The Sox don't train in Miami, but didn't he go to school there? He must have a lot of friends still in the area."

"Good point. I always thought he went because of the weather."

"The weather?" She really was a bit naïve.

"Of course. Who wants freezing winters when you can choose sunny, warm ones and still play some ball?"

He turned onto her street and slowly drove toward her building. "Let's put it this way, Emily. If he were madly in love with a Boston girl, do you think he'd run to Florida for months?" He paused, then answered the question himself. "I know I wouldn't. She'd be too important."

He double-parked in front of her entrance and unsnapped his seatbelt. Emily sat, looking straight ahead and unmoving.

"You're right," she said. "A special woman would be too important. Now, why didn't I think of that? There must be something wrong with me. Maybe I'm missing a gene of some kind."

"The only thing you've been missing is personal time for a personal life." He reached over to unlock her belt and walked around the car, providing minimal assistance as she exited. Then he retrieved her violin from the trunk.

"Thanks," she said as he returned. "I wasn't thinking about her."

She rested her arm on his as they walked through the front doors and to her unit—a small act of trust that warmed him. Emily was a beautiful woman—talented, smart, loving and different. He liked different, and he wanted to know her better.

She turned toward him at her door, looking up, her eyes, dark, shining and reflecting something he couldn't quite label. Curiosity? Longing? He saw a question in those lovely eyes and leaned closer to answer it.

She sensed his intention, his nearness, and felt his lips press against hers. Tasting with small touches, slowly sampling. Shivers swept through her, something delicious, an unfamiliar desire in the pit of her stomach. She stretched taller and gave herself freely to his touch.

Instantly, his feathery pressure increased as his mouth covered hers fully, his tongue moving back and forth on her lips. She parted them, and he leaned closer as she returned his exploration with one of her own. Tongues blending, kissing, exploring, then softening. A nibble at the corner of her mouth, a nibble on her earlobe. That frisson of desire came again. Her breath caught, came in gasps as she finally pulled away—and simply breathed while holding his gaze.

"You mentioned something about my personal time," she said quietly, "the lack of it. Maybe staying home for a while will be a blessing in disguise."

"I hope so," he whispered.

She traced the outline of his mouth with her fingers. "Your lips have a fine talent for tuning things other than an oboe."

Peals of his laughter rang though her hallway. "Too bad I'm double-parked."

"Maybe that's also a blessing—for tonight," she replied, "while I adjust to this period of staying home and being idle."

"You'll figure it out." He kissed her again, quickly this time, before she went inside and took off her coat. From the hallway, she heard, "Lock up, Emily."

Right. She turned the tumblers. "I'm all set."

"Good. I'll call you tomorrow."

##

Idleness was definitely not on Emily's agenda. Surely, despite the hand splints, she could be useful somehow, somewhere.

Her first call the next morning was to Peter Corell, still the director of the Boston Youth Symphony, the same group that Emily, herself, had happily played in during her high school years before being invited to her first summer at Tanglewood.

He greeted her with enthusiasm and reminded her that "even in our…uh…rarified world, gossip seeps out. How are you holding up?"

Her huge sigh of relief surprised her. As did her incipient tears. A colleague. No judgement. No criticism. Simply sincere interest.

"When this is over, Maestro, I'm determined to be less of a workaholic," she said. "In the meantime, I'd like to volunteer with any of the youth groups somehow, perhaps as a coach for the string section or maybe for an individual student. In whatever way you can use me." She inhaled and slowly released her breath. "I simply must stay professionally involved."

"Very understandable," he replied. "And much appreciated. We'd love to have you on board. So here's my suggestion: come down on Sunday at 11:00 and visit each group of our young musicians. The Youth

Symphony, Repertory Orchestra, Junior Rep, String and even the Petit Ensemble of our youngest group of seven to ten-year-olds. I'll give the conductors a heads-up about you stopping in."

As though a warm breeze were instantly lifting her, Emily wanted to fly like a bird on wing. Yes!

"I look forward to the visit and to catching up with you this Sunday," she said before disconnecting.

She'd reached out, and taking the first step had paid off. Her situation didn't have to be a secret. In fact, wasn't a secret anymore, so she had nothing to hide. Abruptly, she began to wonder about her colleagues in the Boston Symphony. She'd been so enticed by Scott and the Doctor's Orchestra, she hadn't thought to connect with her own friends.

Friends? She paused. Time did not stand still. Maybe she'd once had tight ties with a group of string players, but these days, summer reunions with those who visited Tanglewood were the best she could expect. She searched for the current list of Symphony musicians and began to smile. Diane Gilbert, violin; Paul Fanning, cello; Carolyn Honig, violin. She reached for her phone just as a text from Scott came through.

How's your day so far?
Happy to say I'm not idle! Call me later to talk.
Will do.

By the time she spoke with Scott later on, she hoped she'd have more good news. She glanced at her hands, thinking wryly how her definition of good news had changed so quickly. Two weeks ago, good news meant playing a solo concert with an orchestra. Now it meant an opportunity to coach youngsters without pay. Normally, not an issue. But for a long-term plan…she'd have to come up with something salaried if neither of Scott's treatments worked well enough.

Treatments. Either total rest for months and splint-wearing with no guarantee of complete recovery. Or surgery—actually two surgeries on her left hand simultaneously—and the confidence that the pressure had been relieved. Then back to almost normal use somewhere between three to six months. But did normal include playing the violin professionally? No one could make that promise.

In addition, Scott wasn't pushing her in the surgical direction. Actually, he wasn't pushing her in either direction, at least, not yet. Maybe he deserved a gold star in psychology. He'd given her all the details of both possibilities, as well as the time and space to decide—to wrap her head around having the surgery.

She chuckled in appreciation of his tactics as she booted up her computer to do some research. Sure, she'd heard cruising the internet for medical research was a bad idea, but she'd consider it her second opinion.

An hour later, after slowly tapping each key for her search, she knew that Scott was right. There were no absolute guarantees, but she'd made her decision. She'd tell Scott tonight when he called. In the meantime, she'd reconnect with some old friends. And hope for the best on both counts.

CHAPTER EIGHT

"There's now an open warrant for the arrest of Larry Gaines." Lisa's voice held a note of steel when her call came in that evening.

Emily's stomach tightened, however, and she was happy not to have eaten yet. The aroma of her grilled cheese sandwich, which had been so tempting a minute ago, now made her nauseous. She plopped onto a kitchen chair.

"Good God, Lis. With everything else going on, I'd almost forgotten about him. An open warrant? Does that mean the officers couldn't find him at his address?"

"It certainly does. And there's no forwarding address, so that's where he still lives. Now if he's stopped for a traffic violation or anything else, however, there will be a computerized record for the officer to see when checking his background."

"And they can bring him in," said Emily softly. "So sooner or later...he'll be caught."

"Unless he's out of the country," said Lisa. "But yes, sooner or later, we should have him. I sure hope we can recover your money, Em, and that he didn't stash it someplace overseas."

"That's the notion that makes me even more sick than I already am about this. I need that money to help fund a new violin. I'll have to return Joy soon."

A telling silence filled the line.

"What are you talking about, Emily? Return Joy? A new violin? What's going on in your head?"

Lisa, the lawyer, always had two strategies for questions—either pointed and direct or open-ended. It was a knack, a talent. As a child, Emily could never hide anything from her sister. Lisa always figured it out. Nothing had changed. Today she was using the open-ended technique.

"It's really simple, Lisa. After a lot of tests, research and discussion with Scott, I've decided to have surgery and hope for a great outcome. Scott's office will let me know the date, but probably in a week, two at the most."

"Surgery, Emily? Are you sure?"

"If you're asking for guarantees that I'll be able to tour again, the answer is no. I don't have any."

"But your current state isn't working either," Lisa murmured. "We are all such high-energy people, this lying around must be killing you."

"A-a little," she admitted.

"I insist you come home for your recovery. Scott can visit if he wants to. At least, that's the way I'm reading the tea leaves right now."

"Thanks. Thanks a lot. I love you. Lis."

"Right back at you, sweetheart."

Despite the love and Lisa's excellent tea reading, Emily wasn't ready to confide. Her relationship with Scott was too new, too precious. Actually eye-opening to her!

"So coming back to the new violin," said Emily. "After the surgery, even if it's very, very successful, I've got to be open-minded about my future. All I know is that the violin must be part of it, but I don't know in what way yet."

"You'll figure it out. Just be sure to take appropriate safety measures, no matter where your career may be heading."

"For sure. And I'll accept your surgical after-care. Glad my suite's still available." She sighed deeply. "I really love being back in town."

"We love it, too. Mike's very proud of you, but he's never happy when you're traveling."

"Mike wants me to be seven years old forever!"

Lisa burst out laughing and agreed. "I'll be sure to relay that message," she said, before hanging up.

Emily took her time eating her now-cold sandwich, and began taking stock of her kitchen and apartment, along with her life. She needed to get herself organized. *Lists.* Lists always worked. Grabbing a pen and paper, she created several categories: music and career, medical, everyday living. As she reread what she'd written, she felt her heart beat faster. Scott appeared everywhere in her life.

She paused, then sat in wonder as she recognized the message. "Put my name at the top of that friends' list," he'd said the night he took her home after one of his rehearsals.

One of these days, she'd probably tell him she had.

##

On Saturday afternoon, Emily stood outside her building, waiting for Scott to pick her up. He'd invited her to go with him and three others from the Doctors' Orchestra to a local nursing home, where they'd be performing as a woodwind quartet for the residents. She was expecting it to be interesting. It wasn't exactly a romantic date, but being with Scott was exactly where she wanted to be.

The sun shone brightly through the newly bared trees, and standing outside today was no hardship. A just-right cool day. She took a moment to appreciate her lovely, tree-lined street of historic homes, with nearby shopping, and within a very walkable distance to Boston Common and the Public Gardens. Lucky her to have found a safe, snuggly place to call home.

At least, for now. She wondered if unemployed musicians could afford to maintain a spot here. *Don't go there. Don't borrow trouble.*

Her phone rang. Jen began speaking immediately after Emily's greeting.

"You were missed this morning at rehearsal. Everyone wanted to know where you were. You should have come when I asked. We needed another sub."

"And good morning to you, too," said Emily. "Sorry to disappoint you."

She spotted Scott's black SUV rolling toward her, waved and stepped closer to the curb.

"Scott's here, so I've gotta go."

"Scott? Nice. I'm glad your social life is picking up." She laughed. "I'm glad you have a social life at all!

"Think about joining the chorus," Jen said. "The director asked me if you'd be interested. He loved not only your voice, but your professionalism. Your ease on stage."

"I guess no experience is wasted, huh?"

"I guess not. But it's a wonderful idea, Emily. So think about it."

She had so much to think about these days. "I'll definitely put it on my list, and tell him thanks. But I'm not committing to anything until after the surgery. I have to discover if…"

"I know. I get it, but keep an open mind."

Disconnecting, she quickly stepped to Scott's vehicle and opened the door. "Hey, I did it myself!"

His deep chuckle sounded like music to her. "You sure did. My one-armed powerhouse."

"A right-handed powerhouse." After getting in, she said, "Let's see if I can latch the seatbelt." She maneuvered it, heard the click, turned to him and grinned. "What did Gail call it? Oh, right. Activities of Daily Living. I'm a success. She'll be happy."

He leaned over and surprised her with a kiss. "What about me? I'm happy, too. You're my star patient."

"Well, this star patient wants to do everything possible to maximize her recovery."

Scott waited, then pulled out into the light traffic on her street. "Just follow directions, Em. I'm glad about your decision for surgery, but forget about being a diva again post-op; you need time."

A diva? A prima donna? Is that how he saw her? "I'm pretty sure you just insulted me."

"What? What did I say?" He turned his head toward her, and his blank expression reinforced his befuddlement.

"I've worked very hard, Scott," she explained. "I've tried to stay as grounded as I possibly can, so I don't consider myself a diva. Or a goddess. And I'm not a spoiled brat." But the afternoon had dimmed. Just when her heart had opened, had welcomed something special…

"I'm so sorry, Emily. That's not what I meant at all. I think you're perfect the way you are!"

"Perfect? Now you're talking!" Her spirit soared. Of course, she wasn't perfect, but nothing could have soothed her ruffled feathers more than the sophisticated physician looking like a remorseful boy.

"The way I see it," he said, "is that divas turn a black-and-white world into technicolor. They have that something extra that goes beyond an otherwise talented person. A style, a special measure of drama or technique or skill. Not a spoiled brat."

"Wow. You sound as if you've thought about this subject, and with an explanation like that, of course, I forgive you." But her imagination started spinning in different directions until she came up with a theory.

He reached for her hand, connected with the splint and walked his fingers toward hers until they interwove. "Are we good?"

"We're good. But tell me, who called you a diva or is it divo for a guy?"

"How quickly you forget about the rap surgeons have for our God complexes."

Was it only two weeks ago that she'd referred to him as bossy and Lisa had dismissed him as a typical surgeon with one of those complexes?

"Guilty as charged. So I owe you an apology, too. Seems no one likes to look beyond the façade."

He turned into a parking lot and pulled into a visitor's spot. "The public is paying a fee for the diva. Whether it's a concert or surgery. They don't want to know more than that."

She could have argued but wasn't sure she had solid ground. In the end, after the accolades, fans went back to their own lives, where they were center stage and didn't think twice about the violinist who was dashing for the next flight. Maybe Scott was right, but if so, she'd chalk it up to people being human. As he'd said, they didn't owe her anything except the price of the ticket. Or to him, the cost of the surgery.

Could it be he saw himself in her? Someone who understood that being super-talented came with a price? Could it also be he was attracted to her only because of that common thread?

If so, that wasn't enough, and he was not the right man for her.

Another car pulled up two spaces over. And a minute later, Emily recognized the bassoon player and clarinetist from the orchestra, who waved and greeted her by name like a long-lost friend. She memorized their names now—Ben Graf and Lei Wong—and allowed their enthusiasm to seep into her bones.

"Where's our flutist?" asked Scott, gazing toward the street.

"Janie will be here in a minute. She wanted to run by the hospital first, check on a patient," said Ben.

"Uh-oh," said Scott, "that doesn't sound good. And it's not the sick patient I'm concerned about."

"Yup. She does that a lot. I foresee burnout."

"But you were on-call last weekend, Scott," said Emily, "and you went in several times."

"Janie's not on call," he replied. "She's just having a hard time establishing boundaries."

"Scott's right," said Lei. "There's no emergency today. The hospital is fully staffed, and I'm sure she wasn't called in. Normally, being part of the orchestra really helps with that—the boundary thing."

Scott stared at Emily with concern. "We're no different than you, Em. It's easy to keep riding that roller-coaster if you're enjoying it."

"And then you drown," said Ben. "Doing gigs like today's is great, not only for the audience, but for us, because it gets our juices flowing in other directions."

The men were both right. They'd figured it out. Emily glanced from one to the other. These wonderful musicians, although perhaps not as proficient as she, made so much sense. Musically, emotionally, intellectually. She could learn a lot from them in that last category.

"This is one of the most thought-provoking conversations I've had in a long time," said Emily. She turned toward Scott and took his hand, enjoying the light pressure he returned. "You have great friends, Scott. It's easy to see why you're loyal to the orchestra."

Pivoting to face the others, she said, "So, here's my question—do I have to go to medical school in order to stick around?"

She got the laughs she wanted to hear, then added, "Someone better help Dr. Janie. You don't want her to wind up like me, do you?" She raised her left arm with the splint.

"To solve a problem," said Scott, "you first have to recognize it. Our Janie refuses to—yet. But we won't give up." He leaned in with a quick kiss. "Maybe you'll actually be a good influence on her."

They all started toward the seniors' home, Emily right next to Scott. "Be proud of yourself, Em. You've done a one-eighty turn in two weeks. I have faith you can handle whatever happens."

He paused, and she with him. He leaned toward her, and she saw his intent. No words were needed. His mouth touched hers, and his warm kiss sent a shiver through her.

"Just staking my claim," he joked.

"I see that," she said. "But weren't we just talking about drawing boundaries?"

He looked absolutely crestfallen.

"Not to worry. Where you're concerned, I have no boundaries between personal and professional. I think that ship has already sailed." She locked arms with him. "Let's go. I want to hear some great music."

An excited buzz filled the residents' lounge, where not one empty seat remained. An initial glance around the room revealed a community of every color and background, and Emily quickly picked up an Irish brogue, an Italian accent and Yiddish-flavored words among the conversations. Some ladies wore necklaces and earrings. Truly, a big day for them.

As soon as they were spotted, Emily's crew returned the friendly waves and smiles. She waved, too.

"As you can see," said the activities director who'd greeted them at the door, "our residents are very excited. The Doctors' Orchestra visit is truly the highlight of the month for them. No matter which instruments."

"We've been waiting," called out one lady.

"So, make it a long one. Don't rush away," yelled a spry gent.

A bit startled, Emily realized she'd spent very little time among elderly people. Certainly, she hadn't been privileged to see her own parents mature, and her mom's sisters and families lived out-of-state. Other than Mike's folks, who called themselves "active" seniors, she'd had no experience with this age group. They diffused the air, however, with the same pre-concert excitement as any other audience.

"They're not shy, are they? I hope you brought a lot of material," she said to Scott. "They might be your best audience ever!"

A blond whirlwind ran over to them, instrument case in hand. "I'm here!" she said, looking at Scott, then to the others and back again. "What are we doing?"

"Getting ready to play," he said. "Glad you could make it." He nodded at the gathered residents. "They're waiting."

"Aren't I on time? I never miss, do I? So relax."

Scott put his hands up and backed away a step. Then he looked at Emily and shrugged as if to say, "see what I mean"?

Running, running, running. Emily studied the young doctor as she unpacked her flute and assembled it. She could imagine how the woman had spent the morning so far. Time to relax? No. Too busy. Everything was too important. Sort of like Emily's life. No, not sort of. Exactly like Emily—before she'd returned to Boston. Music or medicine? Did it matter when you strove to be the very best?

Five minutes later, however, the first notes of the woodwind quartet settled everyone down and held the rapt attention of the senior citizens. The music started with familiar classics. Emily immediately recognized the overture to *The Barber of Seville,* then *Habanera* from Bizet's *Carmen.* She sat back in her chair, enjoying it just as much as the residents.

To her surprise, the music turned more contemporary, and she heard the Beatles' *Eleanor Rigby* and Elton John's *Crocodile Rock.* Her feet were tapping. She glanced at the audience. They were into it, clapping along, and joining in with a few words. They definitely didn't hold back! Being part of this enthusiastic audience was fun.

A Gershwin medley followed, and she found herself humming along to *I've Got Plenty of Nuthin'.* Maybe next time, she'd talk to Scott about having the residents participate—sing a few songs, too.

Even though some were in wheelchairs and some looked off into the distance, everyone seemed in a happy mood.

Emily checked the time and was surprised to find almost an hour had gone by.

"And now," said Scott to the residents. "Your favorite part. Are you ready to exercise your lungs?"

The full-throated response filled the lounge. Sounded like a sing-along was coming up. Scott had been a step ahead of her. Emily raised her eyes to him and smiled. He was more than a surgeon. More than an oboe player. He was a person who cared about others— all ages, all genders, all races and religions.

Scott turned to Emily. "Hey, Em? How about leading the group—keeping them together? I'm sure you know all these songs."

"A cold try-out?" she asked, walking toward him.

"I'm not worried about *Take Me Out to the Ballgame*," he said.

She giggled. "I'm not either, so I'll just introduce myself. Okay?"

A thumbs-up sign was his answer and she stepped forward.

"Hello, everybody. You've been a great audience." She pointed at the quartet. "They love playing for you." Their applause came again.

"My name is Emily Delaney, and I loved being part of your audience, too."

A man called out, "Delaney? Like in Andy Delaney?"

"You mean the hitter who tells corny jokes?" She stepped closer to the man and asked. "Sir, how do baseball players stay cool?"

"Oh, I've got that one: by sitting next to their fans!" She high-fived him and turned toward Scott. "Let's do it."

The residents rocked it. Even changed the words from *root, root, root for the home team* to *root, root, root for Red Sox.* Boston in their souls.

"What else have you got?" she asked Scott. His eyes gleamed with pride. "Whatever you want."

"You mean, whatever they want." She turned to the audience. "Requests?"

A hundred suggestions. She kept to a happy beat. "How about, *This Land is Your Land?"*

She was impressed with the musicians' repertoire of songs. Woody Guthrie was followed by three or four other favorites, and the musicians didn't falter.

Finally, it was time to wrap up. "Let's close the show with an all-time favorite of mine from when I was a little girl." In five minutes, she had them participating in a three-part round of *Row, Row, Row Your Boat.*

"A fun ending to a fun afternoon," said Scott later in the parking lot. "You were great, Emily."

A sentiment echoed by the others. "You can join us anytime," said Janie.

"Actually, it's good having a conductor for a sing-along, so all four of us could constantly play," said Ben.

"Thanks very much," Emily said. "You're making me feel part of the music scene, which is reassuring. And as for those residents…? Very worthwhile. A great day for them and a good use of time for us. I guess, in the end, there needs to be a balance."

"Sound familiar, Janie?" asked Ben.

"And that is my exit cue," said the flutist. "See you all on Tuesday for rehearsal."

They watched her leave, no one speaking, but Emily could see those unvoiced thoughts etched on their faces. Concern, but not her concern. She couldn't fix Janie or the world. She had to concentrate on herself.

CHAPTER NINE

At four o'clock the next afternoon, Scott drove to Boston University's Fine Arts Building to collect Emily. The woman had stamina, he had to give her that. Despite everything, or maybe because of everything that had happened to her.

He spotted her just as he pulled to the curb, and just as she noticed him. Waving broadly, she ran over, a big smile on her face and got in.

"A wonderful day, Scott," she said as she buckled up, "but first tell me, did you get all your reading done? Your research? I don't want to hog your life completely."

"You have no idea how pretty you are," he said, "how sweet, and how happy I am to see you so happy." He twisted toward her. "C'mere." He put his fingers beneath her chin and brushed his mouth to hers. Then leaned in more. A real kiss.

To which she responded naturally, with an "umm…" and afterwards, a sigh. She reached over and pressed his leg.

He could have jumped her bones right there. It was getting more difficult to restrain himself every day from taking her in his arms and making love to her. But until her surgery was behind them, and they were on a level playing field, he'd continue to hold back.

"I got my reading done, spent an hour at the gym, did a wash, and here I am—at your service."

"Laundry, too? Wow. You're very efficient, I must say."

"I'd like to be as efficient in finding Jennifer's house."

"No problem. We'll use Waze. I haven't been there often enough to give you directions." She busied herself with her chore before turning toward him again.

"I should confess right now that even after all these years, I barely understand football, and I definitely can't watch them tackle each other. So if you see my hands over my eyes, you'll know why."

"That bad, huh?"

"Are you kidding? Even Lisa hid her face all the time. I'm so thankful Mike came away with only two mild concussions—I'm not counting the tears and surgeries. And I'm so glad my brothers play baseball instead. It seems… safer, I guess."

"Unless you get smashed with a hundred-mile-an-hour pitch, then yes, it's safer."

"Oh, my God. Really?"

He grinned. So easy to tease. "Batters wear helmets, Em. It's a rule. It rarely happens. And now, don't keep me in suspense. Tell me about your day. You looked so happy and free when you ran to the car."

"It was great! As good as yesterday with your woodwinds group. I couldn't have asked for a warmer welcome from Peter Corell, the director of the Boston Youth Symphony. So many memories returned—I used to love Sundays. And today, I revisited all the groups I played in, starting with their string orchestra, to junior repertory, to repertory and finally to the most advanced group, the Boston Youth Symphony."

She sounded satisfied, almost elated. Which made him feel hopeful that whatever lay ahead wouldn't beat her.

"I assume each group has a musical director?" he asked.

"Yes, definitely. Peter had forewarned them and they didn't mind me being there. They know who I am, and trusted me to help coach their students. No, they didn't mind."

"Did the kids ask about your hand?"

She hesitated. "Actually, Scott…they didn't. They just accepted it. Interesting that what is such a big deal to us seemed like nothing to them."

"I think kids are like that sometimes. As long as their world is intact, they don't get too upset. Did you enjoy the day enough to make a return visit or two?"

She nodded. "It also occurred to me that I've been too busy to be bored since the night of my concert. The night we met each other." She turned toward him. "A lot of that is thanks to you and your orchestra. You've been amazing, Scott. I don't know how to thank you for everything you've done."

"My pleasure, honey. And while we're on the subject," he said, choosing his words carefully, maybe preparing for that level playing field, "my motives were not all one-sided. I wanted to get to know you better."

A quick glance to his side showed her complexion pinking up. "I think I've figured that out, Scott. And I also think you've been walking on eggshells around me sometimes." She peeped up at him. "Am I right?"

"If you think I'm going to rock this boat, think again."

"A man of honor," she said, amusement lacing her tone. "one of a kind." She started to hum *The Impossible Dream* from Man from La Mancha.

"Whoa! Don't go overboard," he replied, as he turned onto Jennifer's street in South Boston.

She stopped humming. "It's on the right, about halfway up the block."

"Thanks." He found a parking spot—easily in this neighborhood. "Ready?"

She put her hand on his arm. "Before we go in," she said, facing him again, "I want to tell you something. These last couple of weeks have been great—filled with musical distraction—but I have to be honest with myself. My-my professional solo career might be over. I don't know how I'll be earning a living yet, so I need to build connections in the Boston music world." She inhaled deeply, then said, "Will anyone want to hire a washed-up violinist? I couldn't even demonstrate the musical passages for those kids today."

His heart almost sank. The whole situation had finally punctured her confidence. He'd heard her uncertainty, her fear, but never before had he heard bitterness or self-pity. Until now, she'd handled herself like a champ. He covered her hand with his and let it remain there.

"You'll know the answer to that sooner rather than later, sweetheart."

She held his gaze, curiosity lighting her face.

"I checked with the scheduling department earlier, and you're booked in for this Thursday morning." Her fingers curled into his, but she didn't speak. "Are you okay with that? Do you have some kind of conflict?"

She shook her head. "No, not at all. I'm just digesting the reality. I—I think I'm actually happy. Let's get this show on the road and see what happens next."

"What's happening next is that I'm going to kiss you." He leaned toward her and followed up. Her response sent his pulse racing.

She could barely recognize Scott behind his mask and scrubs, and with his take-charge demeanor in the operating room. Only his blue eyes reassured her. He'd visited her in pre-op along with the anesthesiologist and his third-year resident, who'd be assisting with the endoscopic surgeries, the less invasive procedure option—and one that Scott was well-trained in performing. To her surprise, and despite the activity in the room, a total sense of calm filled her. It was time for the next step. Being in a holding pattern had become wearying and worrisome.

It was over in thirty minutes, and she was wide awake, having chosen a local block instead of general anesthesia. Her hand and wrist were totally bandaged in soft gauze. In recovery, the first person she saw was Lisa, and behind her stood Jen. Both sisters radiated their love and support. And advice.

"We're not going through this again," Jen said, bending down to kiss her, "so you're to follow doctor's orders to the nth degree."

"She's coming home with me," said Lisa. "I've got an eagle eye."

"Excellent," said Scott, walking over with no mask, no scrubs, just his white doctor's jacket. "Because this doc has a lot of orders."

Emily ignored his words and just drank him in, so handsome and confident, with a spring in his step.

"Good morning, ladies," he said, but his eyes focused only on her.

"Hi," said Emily. "You blew me away in there, authoritative but calm. Kind of like Andy, before he hits it out of the park."

She received his total attention while he ignored the chart in his hand—her chart. An irresistible smile traveled across his face. "I'll tell Andy what you said the next time I speak with him. Hey, I'm a power-hitter, after all."

Her sisters chuckled, but Emily just smiled and absorbed the action around her. Who knew that this surgery would put her in such a good mood?

Scott focused on her chart. "Looking good, Em. And I agree with Jennifer. Once is enough—for me, too. But what a champ you are—the best patient I've had today."

"The only patient," Emily retorted, "so far. You can't fool an early bird."

"Stick around for about an hour, and then, Ms. Early Bird, you can fly this coop. But first...did I mention post-op directions?"

She shook her head. "But I figured."

"Ever hear of P.R.I.C.E.?" Scott asked.

Lisa groaned. "Here we go again. I'm an expert on it. Her hand will be protected, raised, iced, compressed and elevated. Not to worry!"

Emily couldn't miss the grateful smile he bestowed on Lisa. "Thank you. I'd stay with her myself, but I've got other surgeries already scheduled."

"Doc, we've got this covered." Jen chimed in.

Scott glanced from one sister to the other. "I wouldn't bet against you, that's for sure. But there's one more thing." And now he looked at Emily.

"You'll be feeling better rather quickly, but I swear if you take Joy out of the safe to play her, I'll take her to Chicago and return her myself."

Astounded, Emily couldn't produce a word.

"I know you, sweetheart. You'll promise yourself ten minutes. But that will lead to an hour. And who knows how much more. So, no. No playing yet!"

"When?"

"It depends on your recovery." He walked closer to her chair. "I put a hundred and ten percent into handling my part, so now you need to do the same with your part. I want to hear you make music again, Emily. Very much. So let's not mess it up."

"You sound like—like we're a team or something."

"We definitely are, particularly in this situation," said Scott, capturing her gaze with his. She understood immediately and smiled to herself. Other situations, too.

"You'll be using a knife and fork before Thanksgiving," he said, preparing to leave the group. "Only two weeks off now, I'm told."

Lisa glanced swiftly at Emily and then back at Scott. "We have a seat at our table for you if you're available for the holiday. And if you can stand the noise."

"Lisa! Thanks. What a great idea," said Emily, reaching for him. "Please come, Scott, or are you going home to Pennsylvania?"

The delight on his face matched her own sentiment. "Thanks very much. I'd love to, but with a caveat. I'm on call that weekend, so I may be in and out, running to the hospital."

"Your place is reserved," said Lisa.

"Thanks. I'll call you tonight, Emily." And he was gone.

##

"That man is crazy about you," said Lisa as they waited for the discharge papers.

"I think so, too," said Emily. "And it's not one-sided, although it does feel lopsided." She sighed. "I'm hoping to pull my own weight very soon. I've been depending on everyone for help. Scott has been s-o-o very considerate, always there for me…and I've done nothing in return. Somehow, I don't think that's how relationships are supposed to be. I need to get back to my old self."

Jen hugged her. "There are no blueprints for relationships, Em. No 'supposed to be's.' Mike fell in love with Lisa as soon as she walked through the front door on Hawthorne Street. He took one look—and whammo! That was it. All of eighteen years old. Man, was that something."

Their business done, they left the hospital, and then Lisa reminded them about Doug and Jen.

"The guy never gave up. After five years, he moved back to Boston, lock, stock and barrel and knocked down every door until she trusted him. And now look! A wonderful life with two adorable children."

They reached Lisa's car on the first floor of the garage, where Jen was about to wave them off and continue to her office, but Emily stopped her.

"You're wrong. It sounds like a blueprint to me. Both your husbands were crazy about you and wouldn't take no for an answer."

"The truth is, Em," said Jennifer softly, "we were crazy about them, too."

"Regardless of the issues we dealt with," added Lisa. "Mike and I had plenty of those."

"I know you did," whispered Emily, drinking in the beautiful faces she loved, and remembering how unexpectedly Lisa and Mike had became parents to the rest of the brood. "Through the bad times and the good times, however, we had each other. Remember?" She started to sing their theme song, *Stand By Me.* Ben E. King. And her sisters joined in immediately. As long as they stood by each other, they'd make it.

A smattering of applause surprised them. In a parking lot? But yes, a few onlookers had stopped to listen. Emily showed off her bandaged hand.

"Good luck," she called.

"Keep on singing," said one of the women. "You reduced my stress!"

"That's what music is all about," Emily replied with a smile. She looked at her sisters. "I think we can go now. My stress is gone, too!"

As early as the next day, not only her stress, but a majority of the pain and tingling in her fingers had disappeared. Maybe Scott was a magician after all. And maybe, if this rate of healing kept up, she'd be back playing the violin sooner than she'd thought.

Not with Joy. Of course not. She'd reconciled herself to that notion. The amazing Joy must be seen and heard. The words haunted her, but she had to admit their truth. She took comfort knowing that any professional violinist would love and care for her as much as Emily had. At least, she hoped so.

Sitting up in bed, she looked around at her girlhood room. Just a few pictures of the family hung on the walls—no more posters of the greats—Perlman, Heifetz, Stern, Menuhin and the women, Midori, Anne-Sophie Mutter. How she used to lie in bed and dream of joining their ranks. And for one brief shining moment…she had. She'd reached that impossible dream.

But now she needed a variation on that theme. Another dream. But a possible one.

She heard footsteps, a knock. Mike's voice.

"Are you up?"

"Come on in."

His dark eyes assessed her, glanced at the bandaged hand. "Hurting?"

"Not really. At least, not in comparison."

"Good. I'm going to fatten you up. French toast is on the menu as soon as you get downstairs. I read that instruction packet. Activities of daily living. Using a knife and fork is one of them."

"So soon? I don't want to screw things up. Scott would kill me."

"From what I hear, Scott's not doing anything at all like that with you. Don't wait for Thanksgiving. Bring him around sooner."

She swallowed a giggle. "Like tonight or tomorrow?"

"Exactly. I've been left out of this particular meet-and-greet." He stepped closer. "And I don't like it!"

She leaned back on her pillow. "Love you, Mike." She gestured around the suite. "I was just thinking about…when I lived up here. Life was in flux then. Jen was gone—pursuing her career, the boys were seniors in high school, applying for colleges…"

He lowered himself to the edge of her bed. "The secret is, Em, our lives are always changing, they're always in flux. Our outer selves and our inner selves. Nothing stays exactly the same."

"Do you miss playing?" she asked him.

"Every damn day," he said. "I'd be lying if I said otherwise. But you can't buck reality. I'm too slow, don't have the legs I used to have. Another tackle might have taken me out—in a big way."

"Lisa would *not* have been happy about that."

He took her free hand. "Right. And neither would I be happy. I have too much to live for. But you know all that. I also know you're struggling right now, but I have confidence in you. You'll find your way."

He stood. "One thing I can help you with. If you shampoo in the shower, I can comb your hair. I've had lots of practice with your niece!" He laughed and waved. "French toast is waiting."

Emily watched him leave, love and gratitude in her heart. Mike had always been there for her. Even held her over the sink when she threw up. Oh, she'd been a mess as a kid. No wonder she'd called him Daddy-Mike back then. A confused little girl. Nervous. Frightened.

Until she heard Mrs. Merri play the violin in her third-grade classroom. *Amazing Grace.* Her mom's name. Running a movie in her mind, Emily could picture herself leaving her seat and slowly walking closer, singing along with the violin and ending exactly together on the last note.

That was the beginning.

She glanced at her bandaged hand. *This won't be the end. It might just be different.*

She'd call Mrs. M. later and bring her up to date. And give her a heads-up. Going forward, her devoted teacher would need to change her own life plan, too.

##

When Scott's text came that evening, Emily's stomach fluttered in anticipation of his visit.

"Scott's on his way, Lisa. Maybe I need some lipstick. You keep saying I look pale."

She left the kitchen table and flew upstairs, checked her hair in the mirror, smoothed down her red jersey and paused with the lipstick in her hand. She'd never primped for Scott before, never noticed how she looked as long as she was clean and dressed—which was a big deal before the surgery. Being out of pain by about ninety percent really changed a person's outlook.

Suddenly, she felt a new lease on life—despite being in "flux." The word of the day. According to her brother-in-law, nothing stayed the same, and she'd have to get used to it.

Would Scott see her in a different way now? Not as a patient but as an independent woman? She'd sensed he'd been holding back, as if she were a piece of delicate china.

But she'd held back, too. Confused about his vision of her. Was he simply in awe of her musical ability? Would his attitude toward her change when she was no longer a virtuoso player? Where was he coming from?

Overthinking again. Whether about the past or present, it always stressed her out. Then she'd escape into her music. But no more! She took a deep breath, and told herself, "Just *let the good times roll,* as they say in New Orleans." The city she would have been playing in the next night had she not had to cancel.

She defiantly stuck her chin out, willed the thought away and ran downstairs just as the doorbell sounded. "I'll get it," she called.

And there was Scott. Looking New England-rugged on a cold Friday night with an open jacket and no hat.

"You look amazing," he said, remaining on the threshold, simply staring at her. "Beautiful." He moved a step closer, and suddenly she was in his arms, sharing a kiss that set bells ringing. At least to her.

When they finally parted, she felt her smile widen. "You are a magician, after all, Scott. I feel wonderful."

He looked concerned. "I hope that kiss wasn't just a thank-you."

"Not at all, although a thank-you is definitely in order." She ushered him inside. "I've decided that you and I going to start over."

His hearty laughter caught her by surprise. "Baby, we've already left home plate in the dust."

They went into the foyer, and she closed the door behind them. Lisa and Mike were already there. She watched Scott and Mike shake hands, a strong grasp.

"Look at us," said Emily, taking Mike's hand, then Scott's. "For three out of four of us, our hands have been critical to our careers. Mike's catches and passes, Scott's surgeries, and the fingering and bowing for me." She looked at Lisa. "You're the smart one. All you use is your mind."

They all burst out laughing just as Bobby and Brianna showed up. Scott greeted them like old friends, and conversation flowed as they moved into the dining room.

"Aunt Emily has been very good all day," offered Brianna. "She didn't use her hand at all. Only watched me practice my viola."

"That must have been a treat for her," said Scott, his arm around Emily but his attention on the child.

"Umm...I don't know," replied Brianna. "I'm not as good as she is."

"You're nine years old!" said Emily. "Ask Mom how good I was at your age. I think you sounded great today. The real question is, do you enjoy it?"

The girl wrinkled her nose in thought. "I do like it, but I don't want to practice all day long like you used to. So maybe I'll be a lawyer like Mom."

Mike beamed. "That's my girl. Smart like her mother."

"I'm trying out for the football team as soon as I get to high school," Bobby said.

Mike actually flinched. "Your mom won't like that."

Brianna patted Lisa's arm. "It's still two years away, Mom. Maybe he'll change his mind."

"Fat chance," the boy mumbled, with a glance of appeal to his dad.

"We'll figure it out," said Mike. "Can everyone please sit down before we starve?"

A simple meal but hearty and plentiful. Roast chicken, sweet potatoes, and cole slaw, served family style with everyone passing serving plates and drinks. Emily held up a drumstick with her right hand. "No knife needed. Perfect for me."

"Everything smells delicious," said Scott. "Thanks for including me."

"That was a no-brainer," said Mike, his tone serious.

The men's eyes met in a purposeful stare, and Scott nodded. "If she were my sister, I'd watch out for her like a hawk, too."

"Okay, then," Mike replied, a smile beginning. "We understand each other."

"Oh, for crying out loud!" said Emily. "Can't we just eat dinner without any drama?"

The three adults stared at her. "Well, look who's talking!" said Lisa. "You've provided enough drama lately for ten people."

Emily flinched. "It certainly wasn't intentional. But I'm thinking ahead now, clearing my calendar and ready to take control." She held up her fingers and started counting. "My trip to Chicago with Joy will happen next month after my hand has a chance to heal more. I'm now in the market for a new instrument."

"You know that one month isn't enough," Scott said quietly. "It might take six months or even a full year before you're back to where you were—*if* you get back to that level." He took her chin in his hand and turned her slightly toward him. "We need to deal with the truth."

She liked the sound of that *we*.

Then she heard the silence from the others, sensed their concern. Perhaps she hadn't informed her family of all the unknowns. Turning from Scott, she faced each one by one.

"I do understand the reality of healing. But I also understand another truth." She paused a moment before sharing her thoughts.

"You all know by now—heck, the entire world knows—that I make music from my heart and soul. So I know that in some way, I will continue to make music, continue to play the violin. I may not know where or when or how or even with whom, but I will find a way. I *must* find a way. So, don't bet against me."

Silence filled the room for a moment before Scott said, "Bet against you? I wouldn't dream of it, Emily."

"None of us would," said Mike, "But common sense is required."

"Including less drama," said Lisa. "Boy, did Jen and Doug miss a meal tonight! He could write a new play with the material we provide."

They all chuckled. "So when I-I return Joy to the Strad Society," Emily said, "I want to see if they have other instruments for sale. I'll also visit the luthier we have right here in Boston. I might have one made for me. We'll see."

"How much will you need?" asked Mike, glancing at his wife. "Where's the checkbook?"

Emily shook her head. "Absolutely not. I'm not seven years old anymore, and this is not on you. I'll raise the money. Jen can cash in everything I have. I don't care."

"What happened to the common sense part?" asked Scott with a laugh. "Or do dollars bills really grow on trees?"

She leaned back in her chair, totally relaxed now. "Nope. I have another source. A surprise. I checked my files and sure enough, I did take out a general disability policy when I started touring and set up automatic payments. That's why I didn't remember right away. So that should help." She looked from Mike to Scott. "And I also took out a specialty policy. Lloyds of London."

She watched their raised eyebrows, crisp nods and grins as understanding took root. "Are your hands insured, gentlemen?"

"Definitely," said Scott, "through the hospital and a smaller policy of my own."

"Absolutely," said Mike. "All through the years."

"Now you can relax, knowing I've got just as much common sense as you guys." Sitting back in her chair, she felt like the Cheshire cat and grinned accordingly. Always good to be one up on her older siblings.

"I hate to burst your bubble, Em," said Mike. "But payments are monthly. You're not going to get a million dollars or whatever in one fell swoop."

"Well, I'm not buying a Stradivarius! I'll figure it out."

CHAPTER TEN

Although he'd spoken with her by phone, Scott hadn't visited Emily again that weekend. Between other responsibilities and not wanting to wear out his welcome with Lisa and Mike, he'd stayed away. Now he missed the special anticipation of seeing Emily at his Tuesday rehearsal with the orchestra. She wasn't available. Without Emily in the back of the room, the shine was missing. At least a dozen people had asked for her already, including Anna.

"Better start your goodbyes to that Strad, Anna. Emily's returning her to Chicago next month."

"I see she's not here this evening. Is she getting bored with us?"

He took a moment to answer. "No, I don't think so. But tonight, she's meeting up with a few string players—old friends—from the BSO."

"She can't be ready to play with the Symphony!"

"She's not. And she knows it." But he couldn't dismiss the frisson of concern he had. "She might never be ready, Anna. And then what? Will she be unhappy for the rest of her life?"

Anna patted his shoulder as if she were his mom and whispered, "You got rave reviews on those surgeries. If there is any chance she can perform on stage again, you gave her that chance."

But at what cost if it didn't work out? He smiled at Anna and took his seat in the woodwinds section. He thought back to that first night. In his mind's eye, he saw her hunched over in pain in the dressing room chair. Definitely exposed and defenseless, she certainly hadn't wanted outsiders around.

But she'd needed help. No question about that. He might have been the right guy then, but he sure might be the wrong guy now.

He'd watched a new Emily emerge at that family dinner last week, confident, making plans, not asking advice, seemingly not needing advice. He'd glimpsed the independent woman she'd been before injuries had taken her down. Now he wondered at the amount of independence she craved.

Why shouldn't she keep it light and fluffy with him? He'd made a point of doing that with every woman he dated—until Emily. And now that she was hoping for a comeback of sorts, her focus seemed riveted on her next steps, on her professional future. So where did that leave them? Just friends? Friends with benefits?

He couldn't blame her for ambition. They both had plenty. But if she now viewed him only as a medic, it wouldn't work. Not at all. Certainly not on his part. Dammit! He was letting his imagination run wild.

Checking the rest of the players, he lifted his oboe and sounded the A note. Time to refocus.

##

Emily couldn't get over what a fantastic evening she'd had. Her old friends were glad to see her, commiserated on her situation and included her in the chatter about their musical lives. They'd tried to give her advice as they dug into their dinners at a favorite hangout.

"Don't forget about open auditions," advised Paul, the cellist. "Keep up with the announcements and—

"She's not ready for that," interrupted Diane Gilbert, a violinist. "She's just out of surgery."

"You're both right," said Emily. "I know that, but I so want to get back to playing. It's very tempting to unlock that case, pick up the bow..."

Carolyn Honig, another violinist, had been quiet until now. "Think twice, Emily. Let yourself heal. Being part of a high caliber orchestra is as taxing as being a soloist. The skill set and prep is very similar—only different."

Emily wanted to argue but kept silent.

"It seems weird," said Carolyn, "now that I think about it—the same but different." She took Emily's hand. "You have a solo career. But we all"—she gestured at the others—"are able to play every note, in tune, in time and with a good sound. We read music on sight. We can use every playing technique in the book. Practice time for you and us is about the same. We're never happy because we always think we can improve, so we never stop."

Emily stared at her almost normal-looking hand, which was still sore beneath the skin. "Never stop is right. And look where that got me."

"I think the difference is how far you've taken those skills as a soloist," said Carolyn. "Your extreme levels of speed and agility—which you've maintained—make you stand out from the crowd."

"When you're part of an ensemble," Diane said, "you need to 'play well with others.' You can't stand out."

"She's right," Carolyn said. "And it's not as easy as it sounds. You almost need ESP to play in unison with twenty other people in your section. That's the difference. You can either stand out or fit in." She leaned back. "Understand what I'm saying?"

Maybe they were right. She had stood out. "I don't think I've ever disappointed an audience, but" —she placed her hands on the table—"where does that leave me now?"

Paul broke in. "You need time."

Geez, he sounded like Scott.

"Remember that not every orchestra has a guest soloist at each concert," the cellist continued. "Some performances feature the concertmaster or principal player in solo parts. I've had the privilege myself."

Emily beamed at him. "Principal? Congratulations. It's good to be recognized. I'm so glad you had the time to join us tonight."

"Oh, pu-leaze," said Diane. "Stop feeding his ego. We all have egos, so let's change the subject and the scene." She shifted her attention to Emily. "Let's pretend it's one year from now. Your hands are totally healed and you, through some miracle, have managed to find a wonderful violin that you love. Where do you see yourself?"

Emily closed her eyes. Pictured the last five years—the cheering audiences—the beautiful music—the fabulous orchestras. She'd basked in it all—in the beginning. But somewhere along the way…Now she focused hard, and from someplace deep inside, the truth rose to her throat.

"I-I thought I had everything. I thought playing beautiful music every night would be enough. But—but, in the end, now I understand that it wasn't. Not for me. I was alone and lonely. I missed my family. When you're on the road, no one really cares a fig about you. But I'd wanted it so much.

"My mom and dad…they loved music. So, I played for them, too. Maybe they could hear me…? Or maybe something's wrong with me."

She didn't notice the tears rolling down her face until Diane grabbed a napkin and wiped her cheeks. "Oh, sweetie, you're simply human, like the rest of us. We emote. We feel deeply. All of us. You were simply more driven. You'll find your skills again, but this time, you won't be alone. You've got friends. We're in Boston and not going anywhere, as far as I know."

Emily looked from one to the other. "It's been a couple of summers since we've seen each other, but I'm so glad we reconnected." She raised her glass of wine. "To my lost and found tribe! May the strings never be broken again."

"Hear, hear. Amen." The voices joined hers, and when Emily gazed at each friend, she knew that they—this tribe—had been a missing piece in her life. Maybe that was why she'd loved the summer meet-ups so much. The connections and friendships. They understood each other. Tonight, these peers filled her with hope.

Without planning, she began singing, *stand by me, oh-h…stand by me…*

Her friends joined in with beautiful voices, as good as the harmony she and her sisters made together. Paul's tenor added to the richness.

"Thank you," she said before they heard applause from other diners.

"This tavahn is wicked good," came a true Boston voice from the booth behind them.

"Ya' nevah know what ya goin' to heah when crazy musicians are aroun.'"

Now, she knew she was back home.

##

She slept deeply that night. She slept until mid-morning the next day. Thanks to physical therapy, her neck and shoulder gave her no more trouble. Thanks to the surgery Scott had performed, her hands didn't tingle and throb anymore. When she finally took a shower and got dressed, she took stock of herself, her apartment and tasks for the day. And when she finally checked her cell phone, she saw Scott's text from last night. A text she'd missed.

Everyone asked for you. Call me when you get home—

Well, too late for that. But his surgeries should be over now, and she responded via text.

Scott replied: *Give me ten.*

When the phone rang, she almost didn't hear it over the vacuum and grabbed it on the fourth ring.

"Glad you didn't hang up," she said, leaning against the back of the sofa.

"Nope. That's not my style. I want to hear about your evening, Em, but I'm swamped. I won't get out of here until late. How about Friday night?"

"You sound as if your schedule got derailed. But yes. Come here Friday, and I'll make a simple dinner. I'm cleaning house now. It needs it."

"You're what? It's too soon for heavy work."

"I don't like dust. Time to get back to normal."

Silence reverberated in her ear for a moment. "Have I been talking to myself all month?" Scott snapped. "Or to the walls? Heavy cleaning? Lifting? Maybe it's time for me to step back and let my resident follow up with you. He knows your case. Maybe I shouldn't have taken you on in the beginning. Where's that common sense you boasted of a few days ago? If you screw up your healing, Emily, it's *you* who'll be sorry and it will be your own fault. I'll still be happily playing the oboe—it's your choice."

He disconnected after a quick "talk to you later."

She was stunned. Breathless. Totally in shock, she slowly collapsed on the sofa. A different doctor? That idea came out of the blue. Their first fight. Would this be their last and only fight because…he'd lost respect for her? Because she'd disappointed him? She'd seen spats between the couples in her life. They lasted two minutes, and then the laughter returned. His frustration, however, seemed like more than a spat.

An ache started deep inside, and she wrapped her arms around her stomach. It seemed no matter how she planned, how she tried, she messed up.

Of course, he was right. It had only been a week since the operations. Thumb and wrist. The internal bruising needed to heal. He'd made a point of that— many times. But last night, chatting with her friends had imbued her with such hope, she'd felt she was already on her way.

But maybe not.

She'd have to wait for his call.

How hard did people have to work at relationships? It seemed easy enough. But Lisa had always said she lived in dreamland, and she was probably right. Maybe happily-ever-after wasn't a given. It hadn't been for Emily.

She wasn't a solo artist anymore and might not ever be one again. So that dream was probably lost. On the other hand, was that so bad? Life on the road hadn't been ideal either. With Scott, she'd discovered the beginnings of another kind of happiness. She hoped she hadn't lost that one, too.

She stared at the phone. So tempting. But, no. He'd said he was swamped. Others needed him right now, others who were in pain and hoped that Scott Miller, M.D., could help them. After all, they had dreams too. Perhaps being out of pain was the biggest.

Like Scott's mom. A wave of grief passed through her for the woman she hadn't met. A woman who hurt all the time. Poor lady. No one seemed exempt from misfortune, but everyone had to learn to deal with it.

She would, too.

Emily put the vacuum down and went into her bedroom. She'd clean out her closet, a much gentler task, and donate items to charity that she hadn't worn in a long time. Maybe she'd discover a shopping trip was in her future. That could be fun.

Sliding the door open, she glanced to the right and for a moment was jarred at the row of long dresses. Concert dresses. Performance dresses. Classically simple in muted colors, a reminder to the audience that *she* wasn't the star of the show. The violin was.

Brushing her hand over the garments, she wondered if she'd ever wear them again.

She had warned her family and Scott not to bet against her. But how could she really know? In the end, she chose three dresses to keep for herself. Other women would enjoy wearing the rest.

##

At seven-thirty that evening, Emily heated a frozen dinner and threw out half. She checked her email, caught up with the news and glanced at the clock every five minutes. At nine-thirty, her chest ached. He wasn't going to call. How swamped could he really be? How angry? Was he still at the hospital?

At ten o'clock, when she was tired of staring into space, she texted him.

Can u talk?

Later.

She hung onto the word as a promise. And when her cell rang at eleven, she grabbed it.

"I'm sorry, Scott—I'm an idiot."

"Me, too. And you're not an idiot. You're just impatient. I can't blame you for that. I'm going to remind you just one more time, and then not say another word. If you abuse your hand, scar tissue might overgrow, and you'll be back where you started."

Dismay filled her. "What? Can this happen twice? I don't think I've heard that one before."

"It doesn't usually repeat, but most people aren't as anxious as you to get back to work! And many people do end up with some change to their careers."

"I see," she said slowly, before lightening the mood. "But I can tell you now, I'm not switching to a trombone!" She continued quietly. "So, are we still on for Friday night?"

"Of course, as far as I'm concerned."

"After we spoke earlier, I wasn't sure. But I stopped vacuuming and packed up all my performance dresses for a thrift shop donation. I kept only three."

A long, low whistle came through. "That must have been tough. I'm sorry I wasn't there to help."

"Actually, it was an Emily-only task. Sometimes a person has to face the truth alone."

"I wish I were with you now," he said.

"I do too, but you'd probably fall asleep! You seem to have had an over-the-top kind of day."

"I did. Non-stop. In-patients, full roster of surgeries all morning, then unexpected consults from the emergency room, a department meeting plus regularly scheduled patients. No time for lunch. I'm a bear if I don't eat. I've been told that more than once."

"I'll remember that. What would you like for dinner on Friday? I'll be sure to make plenty."

"Don't cook. Let's go to the North end and grab some Italian. I know a great place."

She laughed. "*Everyone* knows a great place there. Good idea. I'll be ready."

Disconnecting, she smiled at her new knowledge. She and Scott were one of those couples whose tiffs ended quickly. She could trust him. His image came to mind, and she starting vocalizing. *I Just Called to Say I Love You...*

After the second line, she froze, totally shocked at how full her heart was, how she could barely wait to see him again. And how warm and tight she felt inside, deep, deep inside. Her breath caught as she realized the truth: if he'd been with her at that moment, they'd be in her bed.

CHAPTER ELEVEN

From the moment he picked her up, through the car ride to the restaurant and now at a corner table at La Traviata, Emily sparkled in every way imaginable. In her appearance, with those long shiny earrings, in her conversation and in her mannerisms. Her gestures matched her speech. He'd never seen her as lighthearted and had struggled to keep his eyes on the road as he drove.

"So what's a typical day for you at the hospital?" she asked, as a server approached their table and introduced himself. They selected their wine while a roving musician passed by, serenading patrons with *O Sole Mio* on his violin. Scott watched Emily assessing the musician, but she didn't comment.

Several minutes passed before he replied to her question. "My mom had this saying about the best-laid plans of mice and men. Do you know it?" Scott asked while holding his wine glass. "We hope for a plan and then deal with reality. Let's just say, I don't have a nine-to-five desk job."

"To the healers," she said, raising her glass. "Thank you."

"To the beautiful woman sharing my table," he replied, touching his glass to hers, delighted with the deep pink color suffusing her neck.

She met his gaze. "Thanks again...but looks can be deceiving. I've learned how to use make-up."

"You don't use make-up on the inside, babe," he said. "That beauty shines through, too." He reached for her hand. "I like how we fit," he said, glancing at their laced fingers.

A smile began to light her features, then a dimple, and his heart began to race. He wanted her as part of his life—and not as a patient.

"I like how we fit, too," she said, with another glance at their joined hands. "Maybe..." she whispered, "you made a good point the other day. Maybe you really shouldn't be my doc anymore." Her voice had remained quiet, her head tilted to the side as she looked at him.

He homed in on her like a laser. "I'm hoping," he said, "we're on the same page. That you're thinking what I'm thinking. That you want what I want."

She nodded. "I do."

"Em..." he whispered. "I've never been happier...I-I hope..."

Leaning toward him, she whispered, "Yes. Yes. I feel that way, too. Exactly that way. I want you in every part of my life."

With those words, the entire restaurant faded away—tables, diners, staff. Scott stood and walked toward Emily, the only star in his sky. He urged her up and held her in his arms, capturing her mouth with his own. Her lips parted and he tasted her sweetness, heard her satisfied moan. Other appetites awakened.

"Hold on to that thought," he whispered.

From behind him, he heard the violin and recognized the melody. *Love Me Tender, Love Me Sweet....* Timing was everything. The observant musician deserved the gratuity he'd hoped for.

"Seems we have company," Scott said, reaching for his wallet just as Emily's phone signaled a text.

She beamed up at him as she checked her cell. "Oh, a job lead. I'm going to call Paul back, if you don't mind," she said excitedly.

The cellist friend she'd told him about. "Call him," he said. "You don't want to miss an opportunity." He hoped the guy was married.

He watched and listened. Her expression changed as she gathered information and reflected everything she felt. From eager, to disappointment, to renewed excitement, to thoughtfulness. He figured he ought to remind Emily never to play poker! Watching her in conversation was like watching a play. Except Emily wasn't acting. She was reacting honestly.

Something about a music librarian's position with the BSO.

"You said temporary, though, right? For how long?"

Sounded good to Scott. Librarian meant no playing, but a high level of musical knowledge.

"Thanks so much for letting me know about this, Paul. It might work out. I'll let you know what happens."

She hung up, and he sensed her mind racing.

"Amazing how my old friends are coming through. And so fast! They all found out today at rehearsal that one of the librarians is pregnant and needs bedrest now—an unforeseen situation. She won't even be at the concert tomorrow night."

"Your name and reputation alone would open the door, Emily."

"Probably," she agreed. "I don't know everything that goes on behind the scenes, but I do know that without the librarians, the concert would not happen. The scores need to be obtained, marked up and distributed beforehand so the players have time to practice. Then they're collected at the end of the concert series. Lots of other details — the not-so-glamorous kind, I imagine."

"You can handle mundane stuff for six months or whatever. Right?"

"I can handle anything for six months—except lying around and doing nothing!" She took a sip of wine. "I can't believe I didn't think to ask about the salary or the hours. I got swept away by the opportunity."

"You'll find out the details soon enough. In the meantime, the server is heading our way, and I hear your stomach rumbling. Perfect timing."

Her laugh was contagious. "I'm not such a delicate flower after all, am I?"

He shook his head. "Never thought you were. A stubborn prize fighter is more like it. Gets back up after being knocked down. And lets the docs fix her up."

"This prize fighter had the best doc in the world. No wonder she's back in the game." Her dark eyes gleamed and her beautiful smile landed in his heart.

The best doc in the world? Maybe she really believed that. "Let's say, I'm the best in *your* world, sweetie."

Her compliment, however, didn't distract him from her real message. She was back in the game. Her words. He was fine with that now, confident that she'd pace herself until ready to test her limits. And test them, she would. He knew that, and when she did, he would follow her lead, providing support and advice only when asked.

He sighed. A very tall order—for him. But he would try.

##

"I can't believe we found a parking spot near the house," said Emily, holding hands with Scott while they walked. "Our lucky night."

"Any night we're together is a lucky night," Scott replied. "Not too cold for you?"

"Nah. It's supposed to be cold at holiday time. Winter is just over the horizon."

They'd both refused dessert at the restaurant, a tacit understanding that they'd enjoy their real dessert later on.

Now they entered her apartment, and she locked the door behind them. "I have some wine, if you'd like more," she offered.

He took her gently in his arms. "I think I could get drunk enough just holding you in my arms." His voice sounded hoarse, and she looked into his eyes.

What she saw there took her breath away.

"I love you, Emily. It's been building and building. And I've never said that to another woman."

She saw the truth, the love and the yearning. Reaching around his neck, she pulled him closer and kissed him with the passion she felt in her heart. The first note of their own unique symphony.

"Come with me…." She led him to her bedroom and pulled down the bedcovers. "It's been a long time for me, so…"

He kissed her again, and no more words were needed. The touch of his mouth on hers sent her body swirling, yearning …. She pulled off her jersey and heard his sigh, his murmured offer of help. He unsnapped the back hook of her bra as she unbuttoned his shirt.

In less than a minute, their clothes lay in disarray all over the floor as they explored—a touch, a stroke, a kiss. Her senses heightened at the reawakening. He found her pleasure points—across her breasts, her mouth, her ear. His hand skimmed down her stomach to her thighs, and she surged against it.

"Em?" he whispered.

She pulled him closer. And when he entered her—slowly—she stroked the length of his back and urged him on. Her entire body tingled, from her nipples against the roughened hair on his chest to her thighs, taut and tight around him.

She writhed beneath him and he picked up her tempo. Though in harmony with one another, the melody they created was not quiet. It built and built until…Cannons! Fireworks! As spectacular as the climax of the *1812 Overture.*

His breath came loudly, so did hers. "Oh, my God," she whispered, "That was…"

Scott cleared his throat. "So I don't have to ask if it was good for you, too?"

She rolled over, a giggle bubbling up inside. "Guess not. And, by the way, thanks for using protection. Totally flew out of my mind."

"Baby, I visited the drugstore for a brand-new supply almost as soon as I met you."

"That can't be true," she protested. "You didn't even like me then."

"That was frustration. I never stopped liking you, and was always hoping for more than that."

"And I thought you stuck around only because you promised Andy."

She tucked his arm around her. "You want to stay with me tonight?"

"And lots of other nights."

"Good." She yawned. "You know, I've never seen your place."

'My door is open."

"It's your heart that's open. Hands of gold, heart of gold, too."

"Shh. Don't tell anyone. It'll ruin my image."

But no one could ruin his image with her. His big heart encompassed his teenage patient with scoliosis, the baby with club foot, the seniors with arthritis, the older folks he played for at the nursing home, the pros whose careers were in his hands. Scott's heart was on display to all. He was a top-notch surgeon who might be a perfectionist, but was no egomaniac.

She understood that combination very well.

"I just realized," she whispered, "we're a perfect match."

Silence, except for the deep, steady breathing in her ear. She closed her eyes, tucked herself closer to him. Just where she wanted to be.

##

"We're having a Zoom visit with your brothers in a little while," said Mike on Thanksgiving Day.

"Oh, nice," said Emily. "An on-line visit is better than nothing."

"I don't think I've met Brian," said Scott, joining the conversation.

"No doubt you'll recognize him," Emily teased.

"Smarty-pants." His arm came around her and Emily leaned against him for a moment, taking in the family scene.

Lisa and Mike's home, the home of Emily's childhood, was brimming with people and tantalizing aromas. Her stomach was on full alert. She noticed the bouquet Scott had sent, now taking center stage on the extended dining room table. Yeah, he really did like plants and flowers, as she'd seen for herself a few days ago at his apartment.

Mike's folks—Emily called them Aunt Irene and Uncle Bill—had driven in from Woodhaven, where Emily had been born, and were staying the weekend. They'd been friends of her parents, living directly across from the Delaneys on Hawthorne street. Mike's brother's family was sharing the holiday as well, while Jennifer and Doug, with Lily and Laura, rounded out the group.

"Soon you'll need a wall-stretcher," joked Scott, also taking in the scene. "Thanksgiving is my favorite holiday. Thanks for including me."

"And thank you for the beautiful bouquet," said Lisa, "and for putting a blossom in my sister's cheeks. She's the happiest I've seen her since she got home."

Emily felt heat surge. Her face must have been rosier than a tomato. "Lisa!"

But her sister just laughed, hugged her and walked on.

"It's amazing that Mike's not calling a game today," said Scott. "Football is played on Turkey Day, isn't it?"

"I think he insisted on a codicil in his contract about that," Emily said, her eyes following her older siblings. "He's been a family man from the day he came home to us after the accident. He'd never miss Thanksgiving."

Scott's silence caught her attention. "You know, I can't do that, Em," he said, glancing at his watch. "I have to be available today."

"It's different with you. It's not a game. It's about lives. People are in the hospital on Thanksgiving Day. Someone has to be there for them."

He leaned down and kissed her. "I love you, Emily Delaney. I really do."

Whistles and stamping feet followed, along with some catcalls from the gathered guests.

"Oh. My. God." Emily actually stamped her foot, too. "You are all crazy. So I'll give you something else to think about."

Surprisingly, the group quieted down. "I was going to wait until we were sitting at the table, but I have some good news."

"What? You get to keep Joy?" asked Jen.

"Nice thought...but no. So let's take the excitement down a notch," said Emily. "No more lady of leisure, I now have a temp job as a librarian with the Boston Symphony." She had their attention. "I'll be on the phone, acquiring music—purchase, rental or whatever—cataloging the scores and parts. Later on, when my hand's healed more, I might do work for the string section, collaborating with the concertmaster to figure out the bowing, and marking the music. In other words, I'm now a gopher."

"The most talented gopher they ever had," said Jen. "They're lucky you're on their team. But what about the Youth Symphony?"

"I don't think I can be in two places at once," said Emily, "but Peter knows I'm available if he needs another staff member to teach those kids.
They're amazing."

"Congrats, Em," said Lisa. "Points to you... first, for building connections, and now, an actual first step." She turned to the whole crowd. "And now, if you'll all take a first step and more into the dining room...the turkey is ready."

After a lot of hustle and bustle, Mike led them in a prayer of Thanksgiving. It was astonishing how quickly quiet could descend when a serious moment was introduced. Emily absorbed it all, soaking up the family time. Her missing brothers, however, left a hole in the group.

"I want to make a suggestion, and I need your input," she said and waited for their attention. "Have you noticed how our family is growing? We have in-laws to consider, Brian and Megan live out of state, so do Aunt Pat and Aunt Sally, who aren't here today. What do you think if during the holiday season, the Brennan-Delaney family reserves Thanksgiving for our gatherings?"

"Not Christmas?"

She shook her head. "I don't think so. Christmas is more complicated with other obligations. Turkey Day is neat and clean." She paused. "What do you all think? That way, no matter how crazy our lives get, we can count on all of us under one roof at least once a year."

"Smart and perfect," Scott whispered to her.

"I like that idea," said Mike. "Heck, I like the idea of family gatherings any old time!"

Bobby's voice rang out. "We should take a vote."

"Go for it, son."

But he didn't have to go that far. Everyone called out their approval.

"Then it's settled," said Emily. "Thanksgiving is ours! Yay!"

She felt Scott's nearness as he whispered to her, "So, how does Christmas with the Millers sound to you?"

A sudden brain freeze. She hadn't thought that far ahead. But...

"I'd love to meet your family, Scott. We'll work it out." The circle was widening again. That was all.

When he kissed her this time, her heart rate jumped, and love filled her being. The catcalls and whistles, however, surrounded them again.

"Ohh— this is fun," little Laura said.

"I like making all this noise," Lily added, then turned toward Jen. "Mommy, can we tell our jokes now?"

Jen glanced at the children's plates. "A few more bites first." She turned to Emily. "They seem to have picked up the entertainment gene from their uncles. Maybe it's a twin thing. Just wait. You'll go back in time."

"Now, Mommy?"

"Oh, my God. Swallow! Your mouth's full." She turned to Emily. "Raising kids is harder than getting my MBA was. I don't know how Lisa and Mike managed it with us."

Emily didn't have an answer. She was just starting to comprehend the awesome responsibilities her oldest sibling had taken on. Until now, she'd been too self-absorbed.

##

Jen got everyone's attention. "May I now present some Thanksgiving humor from Lily and Laura. Brace yourselves. You've all been down a similar road before."

The girls stood, each holding a spoon in front of her mouth. "These are our microphones," explained Lily. "But I don't really think they make us louder."

"Exactly right," said Doug. "You're loud enough without them, but you're perfect!"

"Thanks, Daddy. You always say that."

Scott's rumbling laughter bubbled up. "Am I at a comedy show or what?"

He looked like a boy, himself. Emily leaned toward him "Laughter is the best medicine of all, huh?"

"Ladies and Gentlemen, including Aunt Emily," said Lily. "Please stop talking. My sister has the floor."

"Gotcha!" Scott murmured in her ear.

On her sister's cue, Laura said, "Lily, how come the turkey didn't eat dinner?"

"'Cause he was already stuffed!"

Howls, groans and applause encouraged them.

"Laura, what do you call a running turkey?"

"I don't know, Lily. What do you call a running turkey?"

"Fast food!"

Emily called to her sister. "I think you and Doug provided the ham tonight."

"Wait, we've got another one," complained Laura. "Why did they let the turkey join the band?"

"Because he had his own drumsticks!"

Mike rose, his cell phone aimed at the children. "Are we done?" He glanced around the table. "I'm sending this video to the boys. They'll love it."

"His boys are men now," said Emily softly. "But I don't think Mike's noticed."

Fifteen minutes later, everyone congregated in the living room with their cell phones to participate in Mike's Zoom meeting. Scott shared Emily's phone. "Oh, good. Brian and Andy are here."

"Yup. I recognize the Texan."

"The Texans are their football team. Brian's an Astro." She called out to Mike.

"First tell them about Thanksgiving. I want them in Boston next time. Brian, can you celebrate Christmas with Megan's family? That would be fair."

"You've got it, honey," called out Brian from his phone.

Then came the business at hand. Emily listened while Mike announced the creation of the *Robert and Grace Delaney Foundation for Children,* whose aim would be to support children who'd lost parents and or who needed assistance to help get their lives on track. From mental health to daycare to legal issues to college scholarships, to summer camp. On a case-by-case basis.

Emily's eyes filled with tears and she told herself to get a grip. Scott's hand encased hers immediately and she sighed, relishing his support and amazed at how in tune he was to her.

"Lisa is drawing up the legal documents," Mike continued. "She and I will be co-chairpersons of the foundation. I'm counting on Jennifer, Brian, Andrew and Emily to make up our board of directors. And I'm counting on everyone in the family to be supportive of this effort.

"So what do I mean by that? While Lisa and I are providing the initial seed money, even a million dollars won't last without being replenished. Therefore, I see a lot of fundraising in our futures. Large and small events. We'll be brainstorming with you all very soon about raising money and other items."

He paused. "Any objections?"

Silence fell over the group, followed by a chorus of "I'm in. Count me in. Great idea." Brian and Megan's voices were loud and clear, too.

"Any suggestions?"

"Right here," said Scott, waving his hand. "A concert by the Doctors' Orchestra could bring in a nice chunk of change. I can facilitate the ask since I'm part of the group."

"And I can vouch for how good they are," said Emily. "Scott plays a mean oboe."

"Let's hear it for the newcomer making the first great suggestion!" said Mike. "Emily, I think you picked a good one. Now, any other little secrets you want to share?"

She brushed his teasing away. "It's no secret that I love you both. Mike and Lisa, you've come up with a wonderful idea. I think Mom and Dad would be proud of us for helping other kids who need it just like we did."

"Hear, hear!" came voices in the room and in Houston.

"But we need more fundraising ideas," called Scott. "Maybe some kind of high-class art auction or dinner-dance."

"You are full of good ideas!"

"Dating Emily was the best one yet."

She totally agreed, but knew that nothing remained perfect and calm. Her professional life was still on hold while she marked time to fully heal. Happily, her personal life seemed to be moving at a fast clip with the person she loved. It hadn't been easy for Lisa — dropping out of law school twice—and it hadn't been easy for Jen, with Doug flying to New York and California all the time, but if her sisters had managed to blend their personal and professional lives, surely she could do the same. Definitely. She hoped.

CHAPTER TWELVE

On the Tuesday night after the holiday dinner, Emily went to another rehearsal of the Doctors' Orchestra. She had her eye out for Anna and waved when she spotted her.

"I'm afraid it's your last time with Joy," said Emily, handing Anna the instrument. "I'm flying to Chicago with her next week. My three-year contract is over. Really over." She'd worked on stepping back. On seeing her arrangement with Joy as a business deal only. She hoped she sounded more convincing to Anna than she did to herself.

Probably not. Starting her new job the day before had helped keep her mind off Joy.

"I'm so sorry, Emily." The physician gently squeezed her arm. "She's special. And I so appreciate your generosity to me. You've given me an experience I'll never forget."

Which is exactly what Emily had tried to do for each member of the audience who came to her concerts. An experience they'd never forget. But now, all she said was, "That makes me happy, Anna. Now play! Play *The Moldau* again. I've been humming it on and off since last time."

She watched Anna reverently take Joy out of the case. "Have you tried to play yet?" the physician asked.

"I'm not in pain, the swelling's gone, and I'm not numb. I'm doing great, but I'm waiting at least another week before I try. That will make it a full month since surgery. Scott prefers three months but…I really can't wait that long!"

"Be careful, though," said Anna. "Don't get carried away. I'm sure Scott mentioned the chance that if scar tissue grows, you'll be facing another surgery."

"Yup, but I'm not thinking about that now. I'm taking it one step at a time."

"Good." She began playing the violin so beautifully that Emily started floating to that dreamlike place she used go to when she, herself, played. A moment later, she somehow sensed Scott's presence and leaned against him.

"Shop 'til we drop," said Scott when Anna had finished. "That's what we're going to do when we search for your new violin."

And this was why he'd captured her heart. He understood her. "I'm going to hold you to that, my love."

"Absolutely. In fact, I've arranged my schedule to go with you next week. We can start the search at the shop that works with the Strad Society."

Maybe he loved her too much. She put her hands on his cheeks and looked into shadowed blue eyes. "It's not truly about the new violin, is it?"

His silence sounded like an admission of guilt. "Is it so wrong for me to be with you when you return Joy? It's going to be tough. No reason for you to be alone. Besides, you'd be on my mind the whole day anyway."

"I'm stronger than I look. Remember? I can handle it."

"But I can't!"

##

She took Joy out of her case. And waited. She gently rubbed her with a soft, dry cloth. And waited. She cleaned rosin from the bow. And waited. She waited through the next weekend when her entire family attended the Doctors' Orchestra concert that Scott and his peers had worked so hard to prepare. The funds they raised would go to a brand-new health center badly needed in a community that had been neglected for too many years.

"They're really very good," said Mike during intermission. "No wonder there's a full house. How much do you think they'll raise tonight?"

"Good question," said Jen. "We all want to know."

"Our foundation is going to need several events a year…."

When her siblings got hold of an idea, they grabbed it and ran. She did too. Her spirit tonight, however, was with the musicians. She took advantage of the intermission and texted Scott:

Wonderful performance. I could feel every note. Need more cello. Is someone missing? Tell your friends they've got new admirers in the Delaney-Brennan clan.

Scotts' reply came immediately.

2 cellists sick. You've got some ear. The show must go on. C u later.

She smiled at his eagerness and at his compliment. Among the elite, however, her ear wasn't unique. As she slowly gazed around the concert hall, the familiarity caressed her like a favorite old sweater. She yearned to be back in its folds.

One day…somehow…in some way…she would be.

She had managed to tamp down that yearning since her disastrous concert six weeks ago, after ignoring the pain for months. She'd held back as much as humanly possible—for her.

Four nights later, at home on the eve of the Chicago trip, Emily waited no longer. She removed the violin case from the safe and opened it with reverence. It was her last chance with Joy, that beautiful extension of herself.

"It's time for a test, Scott."

"Of your skills or my work?"

"Your work was perfect. This experiment is on me. My choice."

But he paced like the proverbial cat on a hot tin roof. The man was nervous—for her sake.

She left the violin, wrapped her arms around Scott's neck and kissed him. "If I'm in pain, I'll stop immediately."

"I love you, Go slowly."

She nodded, returned to the instrument and picked her up. "Hello, Joyful. Want to make some music with me?"

Placing the violin under her chin, Emily reached for the bow and started tuning the strings. As she adjusted the pegs, Scott watched every move.

"It's said," began Emily, deciding on what to play, "that this is what you hear when you enter Heaven. Anna did it justice. I hope I can, too." She raised her bow and began.

The Moldau. The rippling water, the swirls and rapids. The river of loving memory for the composer.

She didn't think about her hands, felt no pain, rose to where the music took her. When she played the last note, her heart beat faster than a hummingbird's, and joy overflowed.

But it was Scott's shining eyes that brought her to a full stop. His kiss left her breathless. "I hope you'll be the strongest string player in the world soon!"

She wasn't taking on the world anymore. "Someone told me there are no guarantees. Remember?" She stretched out her fingers several times and smiled. "No pain. But Joy is going to sleep now."

"And so are we. We have an early flight."

"I get to make love twice in one night," said Emily. "How lucky can one girl be?"

His laughter matched her own lightheartedness. No one was going anywhere alone.

##

At seven-thirty the next morning, she gripped the violin case as they waited to board their flight at Logan Airport. When her cell phone rang, she almost ignored it, her energies totally focused on the day ahead. Only her family knew her plans. And sure enough, it was Lisa.

"Larry Gaines was picked up last night and is in jail now."

"Wow. That's what he gets for speeding, I guess."

"Exactly right. Love those open warrants."

"Do you think I'll recoup any money?" asked Emily. "It might increase my budget to replace Joy."

"Depends if he stashed it off-shore, or if he spent it himself. What an ass. I'll keep in touch if I learn anything else. Good luck in Chicago. I'm glad Scott's with you."

"I could have handled this myself," she said, "if I had to. But I'm glad he's with me, too."

"By the way," said Lisa, "Mike and I will back you with a no-interest loan. So, if you wind up buying a new violin, go for the champagne, not the beer. Nothing too inferior."

Stunned, she couldn't speak for a moment. "Lis! That's so generous of you both. Thank you, thank you so much. Give Mike a kiss for me." She disconnected and repeated the Larry Gaines story to Scott, who'd been openly eavesdropping and had gotten the gist of the arrest anyway.

"As for Mike and Lisa…they still believe in me."

"They're not the only ones, sweetheart."

##

After a quick lunch at O'Hare, Emily called Ann Marie with a heads-up before she and Scott got into a cab and rode to the Michigan Avenue location. A quiet ride, with one hand on the violin and the other gently held by Scott. His presence supported her, and she knew it made *him* feel better to be with her.

Once outside the music shop where the Strad Society was located, she paused, took a deep breath and looked at Scott.

"Ready?" he asked.

"Let's go."

Five minutes later, Ann Marie greeted her with outstretched arms and apologies about the situation.

"Well, I'm sorry, too," said Emily, still clasping Joy's case. "I could have had her shipped, but I needed to return her in person. I couldn't take a chance she'd be lost or damaged." She glanced at the violin. "I love her too much."

The other woman smiled. "I understand. And we so appreciate your care for her."

Emily walked to the attached studio behind the reception area and took Joy out, revealing her burnished beauty and graceful curves. She rubbed her gently with the dry cloth hidden inside the case.

"Shall we have one last performance together, Joyful?" Reaching for the bow, she began tuning the strings. "Let's make it a goodbye to remember," she whispered, "whatever may happen to my hand." She stepped to the center of the room and looked at the others.

"This is Paginini—*Caprice No. 24.*" She smiled at Scott. "I'd memorized it for the Carnegie Hall recital, which, of course, didn't happen."

The woman he loved was amazing. His love, however, soon became tinged with concern as Emily began to navigate music as difficult as a climb to Mt. Everest. She showed more technical wizardry in that one piece than was found in most other compositions. Only a master could play this. Not even Anna, as good as she was.

Regardless of the outcome, of possible reinjury, he couldn't and wouldn't stop her. She needed to play, and for the moment, he simply enjoyed her performance. When he sensed the presence of others in the room, he ignored them. His eyes remained firmly fixed on the woman he adored.

Just under six minutes. As if he'd unconsciously held his breath the entire time, he exhaled with a gust and applauded, watching her bow as though she were on stage. To his surprise, other people's clapping joined his. He ignored them, went directly to Emily and hugged her. "Amazing. You are amazing."

He felt her stiffen. "What? What's wrong?"

"The owners are here," she whispered. "Behind you. I can't believe they horned in on my private goodbye to Joy."

His own anger rose on her behalf. "I'd be happy to straighten…"

"No, no, love. I'll handle it—and here they come."

He watched her grow a half-inch as she straightened her back and pasted a smile on her face. The couple walked right over, seemingly oblivious to Emily's dilemma.

"Emily! That was magnificent," said Margery Robinson. "Why were we told you can't play anymore? I must have misunderstood."

"I wish you had," Emily said quietly, "but I'm afraid not. That was my last performance for a while. I'm healing well but I need more time."

"You couldn't tell anything was wrong," protested the husband.

Emily walked to the table and laid the violin in its case. Then the bow. "I asked for only six months more," she said, pivoting to face the couple. "But you didn't agree. You wanted the Strad to be seen and heard. And of course, that was your call to make.

"So I've kept my part of the bargain." She turned to close the case, then looked back at them. "All I ask is that the next lucky musician to play her is as good a match as I was. She and I…? We understood each other. She became a-a friend."

Beautiful exit line, Emily. Just make your escape. To Scott's delight, she walked straight to him, hand extended. "I'm ready to go."

"We'll give you the six months," called out George Robinson.

Scott caught her as she almost tripped. Heard her whispered *no.* She leaned against him before turning around and speaking.

"You probably mean well, but one goodbye is enough for me. If, in the end, my career has to change…?" She shook her head. "No. Returning her a second time would be too much. If you don't mind, however, let's have Ann Marie contact me in a year about Joy's status."

"Joy? Who's Joy?" asked the woman.

"She's sitting right there," said Emily, pointing at the violin. "My friend has a name, and her name is Joy."

##

She held it together until they reached the corner. "Let's go right home, Scott. I-I just don't have the heart to go back in there and look for another instrument, even after they leave the shop."

"Whatever you want, Em. No rush."

"I guess I'm being foolish," she said, "since we're already here at one of the premier violin stores in the country, if not the world."

"We can visit again, babe. It's a direct flight from Boston, and… speaking of…aren't there significant violin haunts at home?"

"Yes, of course. In fact, several, considering all the musicians there…"

"Thanks to all the medical folks," he said, grinning. "Did you know that over seventy percent of doctors have received musical training? There's a real connection between the two."

She knew he was trying to distract her. So understanding. So not an egomaniac. So perfect for her. "Stop walking," she said. "Just hold me tight."

"My pleasure," he replied, complying with the request.

She tilted her head back, looked into his clear blue eyes, and saw all the love she'd ever need. Love that didn't come from a standing ovation, or from her sisters or from the everlasting memories of beloved parents. She didn't need to travel the world. What she saw in his face was the love she'd yearned for without knowing it. A love she could count on for the rest of her life. No matter what.

She stroked his forehead, cheek, lips. "I love you, Scott David Miller. Thanks for sticking around after a terrible beginning."

"And I love you, Emily Grace Delaney. More than I can put into words on a chilly Chicago street."

She laughed, her heart lighter than a breeze. "It's a sunny day. I don't feel the cold at all."

"Okay, then," he replied, with a determined look on his face. "A minute more won't matter."

To her astonishment, he dropped to his knee and took her hand. "Emily Delaney, will you…"

"Yes!!"

Then she was in his arms, being swung around like a child, happiness zooming in every direction. And a small crowd cheering at the drama.

"Wave to the audience, Em."

"Are you kidding? I'm going to take a bow! And you are, too."

He danced in a tight circle, Rocky-style, with his arms up in victory. "I won the match!"

"Or you've met your match," Emily said. "Now, let's go home."

"Now we have two big items on our shopping list," said Scott, "a violin and a ring."

CHAPTER THIRTEEN

They caught an earlier flight back than planned, and she called her brother, Andy, first—he deserved the honor—and was rewarded with the heartiest of congratulations.

"Actually, put Scott on the phone. I should congratulate him on winning you over. Just remember, I'm taking all the credit. Without me, you'd both be two lonely souls."

And in that split second, she heard something resonate in his voice, and wondered if Andy had revealed his own state.

"We'll see you during Christmas week," she said, "if you can force yourself to leave fun-in-the-sun Florida."

"Oh, I'll be there. Count on it. Love ya, Em."

She handed the phone to Scott and whispered, "He needs to meet someone."

Scott's smile covered his face. "I agree. Everyone should be as happy as I am."

Her cell rang before she could make the next call. Lisa.

"Perfect timing, Lis. I—"

"Good and bad news," interrupted Lisa. "The creep did open a Swiss bank account while in Europe. And that's where most of your funds are. But there a bit of salvation. He also bought a Mercedes sedan here in the States, which will be turned over to you, as well as some jewelry."

"Give me a minute to take this in," said Emily. "My mind was elsewhere. So…I'll get the value of the car and jewelry. Which I actually earned for myself. Do I have to see him again?"

"Nope."

"Good. Now we've got something to tell you…"

Two nights later, after Jen's concert, where she managed a show- stopper with her rendition of *Don't Cry for Me, Argentina,* the entire family made their way to La Traviata.

"Now that we're all together," said Emily, "I can share the whole Chicago story." She dove into the visit, including Scott's proposal on a street corner along Michigan Ave.

"I'll never forget it," she said. "It will be a wonderful memory forever."

"And we had a busy day today," Scott added, nodding at her.

She extended her hand. The ring they'd chosen, a classic round stone, glowed brilliantly in the reflected lights of the restaurant.

"Her eyes are shining more brightly than the diamond," said Mike, studying Scott across the table. Assessing him. "Make sure they stay that way."

"Oh, for goodness sake!" said Lisa. "There he goes again."

Doug "A-hemmed" and all eyes went to him. "I think I was the first to get that speech," he said, putting his arm around Jen. "Poor Briana. I can only imagine what that will be like when her turn comes."

Mike held up his hand in protest while the others chuckled. "The way I see it, and the way I've always seen it," he said slowly, "is that they're all my children—two daughters, two sons. I couldn't let Robbie and Grace down."

Lisa nodded and patted Mike's shoulder. Jen reached for his hand. Mike's grief had matched theirs.

Emily spotted the restaurant's violinist and waved him over. "Do you mind?" she asked, standing. She reached for his instrument, vowing to make a silk purse from a sow's ear if she had to.

She lifted the bow, and the notes came automatically…the familiar notes for her mom and dad. *Amazing Grace.* The nickname Rob had given his wife. The melody sounded rich and full, and if the violin lacked anything, no one noticed as a solemn joy surrounded them.

When she finally placed the bow down, she lifted her wine glass. "To Mike Brennan, for giving me a childhood full of love and safety, and to Scott David Miller, as we get ready to share an everlasting adventure together."

"A never boring adventure!" added Scott.

##

Six Months Later

She'd learned a lot during her tenure as a music librarian, and surprisingly, had never been bored. She'd made friends and thought she'd earned the respect of her colleagues. On her last day, after receiving many thanks and appreciative compliments, as she was preparing to go home early, the friendly FedEx delivery guy popped in with more packages.

"But this one's special," he said, handing her a box. "It has your name on it with the word *personal* in letters yeah high."

From Chicago. Her purse dropped to the floor as she found a letter opener to slice the packaging. Ann Marie's note was short and simple:

She's not Joy—and not as expensive—but when I felt her lightness and heard her sound, I thought of you. She's a sweetheart, so if you keep her, you can call her Sugar!

She laughed out loud. Ann Marie knew her well, and Emily hoped this one, finally, would be the winner. Scott had dubbed her the "try-out queen" of Boston, because she'd been borrowing different instruments each week to try them out. Well, she was tired of it, too!

With a hopeful heart, she released the violin from its case. A golden burnished finish, instead of red, but beautiful. She lifted her out and did notice the lightness in weight — a necessity to prevent pain in her shoulder. *Now...let's hear you,* she thought.

But not in her crowded office or any of the small hallways nearby. She examined the bow and nodded. A minute later, she stood alone at the back of Symphony Hall. *The scene of the crime.* Her last professional performance eight months ago. But also the night she'd met Scott.

She tuned the strings and said, "Okay, Sugar. Let's see what you've got." She gazed over the empty seats. "Your vast audience is waiting."

In a good mood, a hopeful mood, she started with an étude before going into *The Swan* from *Carnival of the Animals* by Saint-Saens.

A good workout. Ending with scattered applause from the side aisles in the hall. Emily couldn't see exactly who the folks were, but she waved. "Thanks. How did she sound?" she asked, holding the instrument in the air. "I'm trying her out."

A tall shadow emerged and started walking toward her. "She sounded very good, very good indeed. What other pieces did you have in mind?"

At that moment, Emily realized she was speaking to the BSO conductor. She liked him. Cool and professional. Her last solo performance had been under his baton. Most recently, of course, she'd worked with him readying musical scores. He was well aware of her medical issues, gently inquiring about her health from time to time.

Telling herself "nothing ventured, nothing gained," she took a breath and asked, "Is there anything in particular you'd like to hear now?" Just as she was testing out the violin, this interlude might be a test for her.

As though he'd read her mind, the conductor said, "You don't need an audition, Emily. You've proven yourself many times over as a soloist."

"I suppose that's true," she replied, "but my career has changed direction now, Maestro. No more world tours. I'm a Boston girl now. I also limit myself to no more than four hours of practice per day."

He nodded. "Excellent decision. If everyone wised up about injuries, there would be fewer of them."

Her body relaxed, almost as if she'd been forgiven by the Pope.

"What do you want to do now?" he asked. "What is your new direction?"

It was really an easy question. "I must play the violin. I must make music. Whether with a chamber group, full orchestra or a bistro on the corner! She held up the instrument. "I've been haunting stores and collectors for six months trying to replace my wonderful Strad, which was on loan. I think I finally got lucky. So I'm ready to move forward."

He looked her straight in the eye. "A soloist has to stand out from the crowd; an orchestra member has to fit in and be part of her section. She needs great awareness of twenty other players. And she must conform. The jobs are, in reality, mutually exclusive. Have you thought about this?"

She and her friends had discussed this very topic, and she had a great answer for the conductor. "I've not only thought about it, but tried it. Are you aware of the Doctors' Orchestra here in Boston?"

"Of course."

"I've sat in with them a few times—my fiancée is their principal oboist—and I've gotten to know the players." She gazed over his shoulder. "To be honest," she said quietly, "I did give them a few suggestions in general, and some for their string section in particular, which they implemented, but I totally enjoyed playing and being part of the group."

"Can you meet me in my office in five minutes?"

"I certainly can."

##

First, she stopped off at the florist and then at the package store. By the time Scott got home from the hospital, she wanted everything in place.

As soon as she heard his key in the lock, she flew to the door. "We're celebrating!"

"Hey, girl, I do that every day." He reached for her and glanced at the set table—with pretty placemats—in the open kitchen area. "I guess we really are celebrating. But if you buy one more houseplant, this place will turn into a jungle."

"And I thought it was a botanical garden."

He pulled her against him. "So what's the good news, my little daisy?"

"I think I found my new violin."

"No kidding? I'd almost given up on that."

"But I'd like you to hear it before I commit." She stepped out of his arms, reached for his hands and squeezed them. "But that's not all."

His brows rose.

"Scott…Scott… You're looking at the newest string player of the Boston Pops, which is mostly composed of BSO members. I signed a contract for this summer—talk about last minute—and if it works out, I'll get to be part of the BSO permanently. Maybe as a floating string player at first—you know, filling in when needed, but practicing everything. The maestro wants to be sure I can fit in."

His brow creased for a moment, then cleared up. "Ah…no prima donnas need apply, huh?"

"Have I told you how smart you are?" She kissed him. "Life is so good. I'm so happy."

"Congratulations, sweetheart," he said, leaning down to kiss her. "What a coup! And a cause to celebrate. But truthfully, I'll be happier after next weekend. I want us both under one roof all the time."

She smiled and agreed. "Who else chooses a wedding date because the Red Sox and Astros are playing each other in Boston on a June weekend? Only in my family!" Andy and Brian would both be in town, and of course, Megan and Josh would be here, too. A happily pregnant Megan.

"I'm looking forward to seeing your family again, too, Scott. Our Zoom chats are fun, but an in-person visit is better. It's been six months since we were there at Christmas."

"Sure, you think Zoom is fun," he said. "You're hearing all about my misspent youth."

Laughing, she led him to the table and poured the wine she'd bought. "To the Delaney-Miller branch of our families—we're adding another unique melody to the score."

"You're so right. Another unique melody," said Scott, "with major assistance from Rob and Grace, who shall not be forgotten."

Her memories were fuzzy, but it seemed as she grew older, she dipped into that memory bank more, trying for clearer pictures.

"Never forgotten," she whispered. "Thank you, my love."

His eyes gleamed as he raised his glass again. "And here's to all the wicked good times ahead!"

Emily laughed. "Wicked good? For sure, I'll drink to that!"

The End

HELLO FROM LINDA

Dear Reader—

Thank you so much for choosing to read *Heartstrings*, the third book in my brand-new series, *No Ordinary Family*. I hope the story kept you turning the pages as Emily Delaney and Scott Miller figured out that professional success falls short without a loving partner to share it with.

Emily's older brother, Andrew, twin brother of Brian, is about to discover his own true love in the fourth book of the series, *His Greatest Catch*. A power hitter and centerfielder for the Boston Red Sox, Andy has a care-free life, a great career, an off-season place in Miami and siblings he can count on. Until they serve him up at a bachelor auction.

Shannon Murphy Roberts is Andy's old friend from high school who's always had a soft spot in his heart. Now she's a young widow with a small child, back in Boston to be near family—and to resurrect her career as a photographer. After reconnecting, Shannon agrees to "save him" by bidding on Andy at the auction.

Heroes come in many forms, and love has no rules the second time around—or the first time, either. An excerpt from *His Greatest Catch* follows this letter.

You'll also find a second excerpt which shines a light on why the Delaney siblings are *No Ordinary Family*. In *The Broken Circle*—the book that started it all—you'll be introduced to the Delaneys in their growing up years where the spotlight is on Lisa and Mike.

If you enjoyed reading *Heartstrings*, please help others find it so they can discover Linda Barrett books, too. Here's what you can do:

- Write an honest review and post it on Amazon, Barnes & Noble, iBooks, Kobo or any of your favorite book sites. Short is good!
- Keep up with me at my website at: www.linda-barrett.com to find out about upcoming books.
- Sign up for my newsletter on my website.
- Tell your friends! Word of mouth is still the best way to share news about a book you've enjoyed.

I'm sincerely grateful for your help in getting the word out about *Heartstrings* and my other novels, which are listed below and available both electronically and in print.

Thank you very much for being a Linda Barrett fan. I truly appreciate you!

Best,
Linda

.

EXCERPT FROM
HIS GREATEST CATCH
(NO ORDINARY FAMILY SERIES BOOK FOUR)

Robert and Grace Delaney
Heaven
The Universe

Dear Mom and Dad,

Do you know what a shrink is? I visit a shrink every week now, but I don't talk a lot. I'd rather talk to you, so writing is better. I miss you so much. We all do. Can you hear us talking down here on Earth? Emily thinks you can. So, every night, she plays Amazing Grace on her violin. Just for you, Mom.

Dad, remember how you played catch with Brian and me in the backyard every night? Well, now we're

baseball players—we're on leagues every spr[i]
summer. I wish you could coach! Or at least b[e]
stands and see us play.

I'm mostly sad inside, but sometimes, I'm m[ore]
mad than sad. Stupid accident! Stupid ice! Only one
thing is good. Brian and me. We stick together. I'm glad
we're twins.

I love you to pieces. Maybe one day, I'll hit a home
run all the way to heaven.

Your son,
Andy

P.S. I'll write again soon.

Eleven-year-old Andrew Delaney folded the letter and
searched his oldest sister's desk for an envelope and
stamp. He knew exactly where to look. Writing had
become a habit, and he was happy Lisa always had
stamps lying around.

He walked into the hallway and slipped the
envelope amid the outgoing mail where no one would
notice it.

Twenty-one years later...

Boston liked its holiday weather crisp and clear, and that
was just fine with Andrew Delaney. He inhaled the clean
air with a quick nod of approval as he left the printing
shop mid-afternoon and hoisted the heavy box to his
shoulder. He'd become the family go-fer. *Reduced* to
being the family go-fer. According to his sisters, it was
his own fault for being single. He had more freedom to
come and go at odd hours.

He chuckled, recalling how his mock complaints were laughed at by his family. Only his oldest sister, Lisa, had said, "you're not the go-fer, Andy. For this event, you're the *go-to* guy! We want to raise megabucks for the foundation." She still acted like a mom.

He didn't mind being the errand boy for next week's gala at all. The box he carried contained attractive program booklets honoring all donors as well as guests attending the affair, and had his seal of approval.

Any organization raising money for kids without parents would be at the top of the list for him. But this one was special. The *Robert and Grace Delaney Children's Foundation.* He and his siblings had created it in memory of their own parents and were on the board of directors.

He turned the corner and started down historic but trendy Newbury Street toward the parking lot where he'd left his SUV. People roamed up and down the block of brownstones, searching for the boutiques, eateries or specialty shops on their lists. Actually, a pretty sight full of colorful parkas, knit caps and the holiday sound of jingling bells and calls of good cheer. Shop doors opened and closed as he snaked his way toward his goal. Shouldn't all these shoppers be home cooking on the day before Thanksgiving and leave the sidewalks less crowded for him? Ha! Fat chance.

He began humming a holiday tune when the door of an art gallery on his left started to open. Moving to avoid it, he saw a woman trying to maneuver a baby stroller onto the street. He grabbed the door handle and held the door open.

"Thank you," she said, looking up at him. "Thanks a…lot." Her blue eyes narrowed. But he'd recognized her immediately.

"Shannon? Shannon Murphy?"

A smile slowly crossed her face; her eyes brightened. "Andy Delaney! How nice."

"And you're still batting a thousand. You never mixed Brian and me up back in high school," said Andy. "One of the few who didn't."

She pushed the carriage further onto the sidewalk, and he released the door. "Going my way?" she asked, maneuvering the stroller.

"Sure," he replied, not caring exactly where she was headed.

The carriage rocked. "Out, out," came a high-pitched voice.

"Whoa. That's sounds like a command." Andy peeked down at the toddler, noting the same blue eyes as her mom. "Cutie," he said.

"And a handful."

"And how old is this little handful?"

"Two-and-a-half. Actually, almost three. We're doing some errands today, and the gallery was on my list. A quick visit."

"Not a usual place for a baby carriage, huh?"

"Today wasn't usual. My holiday bonus was ready early and I was anxious to pick it up. I work there."

The baby looked at Andy, her eyes narrowing. "Mom-my?" she wailed.

Shannon leaned over the stroller. "This is Andy, honey. Andy is my friend."

"Fwend?"

"Yes. An old friend." She patted Andy's arm.

That's all it took for a change to occur. A smile appeared first, then the toddler raised her arms. "Mommy, up, up."

Once in Shannon's arms, Maddie studied Andy, then looked at her surroundings. "Doggy! Look, Mommy." She pointed, then exclaimed, "Two doggies!"

She wriggled with excitement and caught Shannon by surprise.

"Back in the stroller for you, Maddie. We're almost at the car anyway." She leaned over the carriage.

"Hang on a sec. Let's give her a break," said Andy. "If you balance this box on the stroller, I'll carry her…if she'll come to me." He placed the box, then extended his arms. "Want to see more, Maddie?"

She glanced at her mother.

"It's okay. Remember, Andy's my friend."

Her smile inched across her face. "Up, Fwend. Up. Higher! See more."

Andy grinned back, and glanced at Shannon with his thumb up. "Wow! She's a great kid. Good common sense. Jen's twins trusted everybody. They needed a leash!" Glancing at Shannon's questioning look, he added. "Anyway, that's what Jen said. I'm innocent." He took the child from her mother. "Is this high enough, baby?"

"Not baby. Maddie!"

Shannon's soft laughter got to him. Sounded sweet and familiar. Like in the old days when they'd worked on the school newspaper together.

"Now, I know you're really Shannon Murphy. You always had the greatest laugh. Still do. Family life must agree with you."

The laughter stopped. Her eyes darkened. Something wasn't right and Andy braced himself for whatever she was about to say next.

"It's Roberts now. Shannon Roberts, but family life is only Maddie and me. I named her after her dad." She paused, then quietly said, "Matt died in Afghanistan without ever meeting her."

His breath caught, and Andy automatically took her hand and squeezed it, his heart heavy for her. "I'm terribly sorry, Shan. I see the stories on television…and I donate…but…"

"Yeah. It sucks. It really does. Oh..,Maddie's a wiggly worm, so hold on tight—like when you catch a fly ball at Fenway."

"Got it."

"Mommy…?

"I'm right here. Andy is holding you."

The baby looked down and studied him. "An-dee…"

"Close enough. Do you know more words?"

She nodded fiercely and began singing. "Old Macdonna hadda farm. E I E I O. Cow! Moo moo, evewywhere a moo moo."

"So glad I asked," said Andy. "She could be a Delaney. In my family, everyone sings. It's unreal."

"I don't really know anyone in your family but you and Brian," she said, "so I'll take your word for it. Glad and amazed you both got what you wanted…Major League baseball. What are the odds?"

She gestured down the street. "Are we heading toward the same parking lot?"

"Seem to be," he replied, ignoring the career comment.

They started walking and the box shifted position. Shannon steadied it. "What's in here, Andy? It's pretty heavy."

He sighed. "Those are programs for the big gala we're putting on a week from Saturday night. A fundraiser for the memorial foundation in memory of my parents."

"I've heard about it," she said slowly. "My folks are going. I think they bought a whole table for Murphy Auto Parts with my two siblings and their spouses and of course, my grandfather. He loves to be in the thick of things."

Andy's mind raced like a car at the Daytona 500. "What about you? Can't you come?"

"I-I really haven't been going out yet…" She glanced up at her daughter, who seemed content to watch the world from on high.

"Maybe now's the time to consider it," said Andy, "if not for your sake, for mine."

"Yours?" she asked in surprise. "Mind explaining? Who, what, where, when, how and why?"

That newspaper experience seemed to have stuck. Andy took a moment to consider the details of the dinner-dance that meant so much.

"I'm going to be auctioned."

Her mouth opened and closed. "Could you repeat that?

"Part of this fundraiser is a bachelor auction. The most, and I quote, 'eligible bachelors in town.' Which evidently includes me. Plus a couple of other Red Sox players, a couple of physicians that Scott—my sister, Emily's husband—recruited, some CEOs and other high-profile Boston bachelors. We've got local radio personalities to do the announcing, but Mike will be the general emcee."

"Ah-h. Of course. Mike Brennan, your brother-in-law. How's the quarterback liking retirement?"

"Not retired. Just a change in careers. He's announcing for the Riders now instead of playing. So, whaddyasay, Shannon? Will you save me?"

Shannon remained quiet, but at least she hadn't said an outright no. "And I'll return the bid, of course," he added. "I don't expect you to lay out big bucks for this."

"I hadn't gotten that far in my thinking, but Andy. I'm sorry. I don't go out yet. Can't quite bring myself to rejoin a social singles world. I just kind of stick with my family."

He gave her a moment. "Then maybe it's time to reconsider," he said. "Maddie's almost three now. Is the right time when she's four? Five? Eighteen?"

He sensed her irritation but continued. "Before you know it, you'll be rocking on the porch of an old age home with a basket of yarn at your feet, knitting blankets! Think about it."

Her spontaneous laughter surprised him. Maybe surprised her as well.

"You really painted a picture there," she said. "I've already got the rocking chair. That's how I put Maddie to sleep some nights."

He glanced at the baby, who was sucking her thumb, still content to observe the world from on high. "You and she make quite a picture. A beautiful one."

"Are you trying to soften me up?" she asked, smiling. "Well, it worked. I'll…think about the auction and let you know." She stopped walking and searched her purse. "Here it is," she said, holding up her cell phone. "What's your number?"

Encouraged, he told her and whipped out his own phone from his jacket pocket. "An even exchange," he said, handing it to her. "Since my hands are full, will you…"

"Sure…but don't count on me, Andy. I'm not the same girl you once knew."

##

Shannon's high school memories of Andy Delaney kept her company as she drove up Commonwealth Ave to her less trendy neighborhood and turned onto Birch Street and into her own driveway. The Andy she'd just left at the parking lot—mature, handsome, confident— superimposed himself on that teenager of memory. More wiry and slender back then, of course, and quieter than

169

his brother. He'd matured into an attractive man, still a friendly sort. Of course, he'd always had the confidence a gifted athlete carried. As center fielder for the Sox, his self-assurance could only have grown.

After turning off the car's engine, she opened the rear door as quietly as possible and removed a sleeping Maddie from her car seat, hoping her daughter would remain asleep for an hour or two more. Walking to her front door with keys in hand, she looked with satisfaction at the safe and homey world she'd created for her little family.

True, the clapboard, Cape-style house was small. In fact, it could be called tiny. But it was hers, thanks to her parents' help with the down payment. Not that she wanted to accept help, but her choices had been limited.

Move in with her folks? Stay in Texas on the military base? Her folks were great, but had she given in, she would have lost her independence. Her military family was also great, but too far from Boston. She couldn't, in good conscience, keep a brand-new baby away from all the grandparents. And she, herself, had been an emotional mess.

Her wonderful Matthew, an officer caught in an ambush by supposedly friendly locals. She should have been prepared; military wives lived with that fear every day. But grief had crushed her. She'd needed the love and support of her mom and dad, brother, sister and their families and her Pops.

So here she was, in her own place, with family nearby but not choking her. Life was as good and safe as it could be. Calm. Until a pair of gleaming green eyes popped into her mind. Her recent memory of the past hour.

A glitzy dinner-dance with a million people?

She shivered. No way. She preferred intimate gatherings.

A bachelor auction?

Definitely not her style. Besides, she didn't even own a fancy dress.

Andy had been a friend, but high school was a long time ago. She'd call him tomorrow and hope he'd understand her refusal.

Now she had to bake an apple pie and prepare dressing for tomorrow's turkey. Oh...dang! She couldn't call him on Thanksgiving.

She slipped off Maddie's winter jacket and kissed her soft cheek as she laid her in the crib. "Here's another one, from your daddy," she whispered and kissed the toddler again.

##

"Wow! What a mess. Where do you want this carton?" Andy stood in the center hall of his oldest sister's house on Beacon Street, the house he'd grown up in, not believing the disarray of stuff that greeted his eyes. Boxes everywhere. Papers piled on the coffee table. So unlike Lisa, who believed in organization.

"It's an organized mess," Lisa protested. "I know where everything is."

That he could believe. "What about everyone else? You know, the people who are supposed to help out here?"

"Just label the carton in big letters," she said, handling him a fat marker. "The last I knew, everyone could read."

"Yes, ma'am." He winked and followed orders. "I guess this is why Jen and Doug are hosting Thanksgiving tomorrow instead of you."

"For sure, especially with Mike calling the Riders' game in the afternoon—fortunately they're playing in town—so Jen needed to step in."

He started strolling the room, glancing at the various envelopes and printouts. "Where are the RSVPs?" he asked.

"On my computer," Lisa replied, "based on the mailed responses with payments, each table assigned and labeled. Who are you checking on?" She walked to her computer and looked at him.

"Murphy Auto Parts," he replied. "I ran into someone from the family who recognized me."

Lisa nodded without clicking the keyboard. "They bought a full table of eight, but I think they only gave me seven names." She laughed and shook her head. "I've got those whole-table reservations memorized. The Murphy's run a good business, and we like to patronize locally if possible. The grandfather and father still buy season tickets to the Riders' games and...partial season to the Red Sox." She shook her head in wonder. "I bet that's what keeps the old guy young."

Andy could think of other reasons, like an adorable baby, but kept the thought to himself.

Her eyes caught his. "Is your tuxedo pressed and ready for prime time? I'm betting our handsome eligible brother will bring in a huge hunk of change." She grinned. "We're going to have a great event and a great time."

"Maybe you will," he murmured, glancing at his watch. "Where are the kids? It's three o'clock."

"Always looking for action..."

The front door banged open and noise entered. "There's your answer," said Lisa, rising to greet her children.

"Uncle Andy's here!" shouted Briana. "Good. We're in for some fun."

Lisa's eyes shone. "That's what you're known for, little brother. It's not a bad thing. And they miss you when you're in Florida."

His winter home in Miami was what she meant.

He hugged his teenage nephew, Bobby, and leaned down to kiss Briana. "How about we mess up the kitchen and create a surprise dinner for everyone?"

"Oh, goody!" said Briana. "Those surprises turn out to be our most genius creations!" She turned to Lisa. "Mom? Are we stocked or are we bare?"

Andy was pleased Briana remembered that they used only ingredients already on hand for this cooking challenge. And by her reaction, his sister remembered, too.

Chuckling, Lisa approached Andy and wrapped her arms around him—or tried to. "Oof, you must be working out a lot. If I haven't already said it, I'm so glad to have you home for an extra while post season—even if I have to give credit to this fundraiser. And I hope you'll come back for Christmas this year."

An image of big blue eyes came into his mind, and he almost wished they hadn't. As he stepped back, however, he played it cool and simply shrugged. "Nothing's set in stone." Which was just the way he liked to live. He winked at Lisa. "Flexibility and no commitments. That's the upside to being single. A 'we'll see about Christmas' is the best I can give you."

Two highchairs, one booster seat... Thanksgiving at her parents' home did not resemble the idyllic greeting cards of the holiday. No quiet "please pass the butter" or "the sweet potato pie is yummy" on the lips of her family. Just voices talking over one another, increasing the decibel level with each passing minute.

Shannan sat back at the table, gazing from one family member to the other, loving each of them and happy to be ensconced, but sensing the beginning of a headache as she popped another bit of sweet potato into Maddie's mouth.

Her daughter, on the other hand, seemed to be in heaven, twisting left and right, babbling non-stop to whoever showed an interest. Which meant everyone. And wasn't that the point of moving back home? Security for her daughter, who needed loving people in her life.

Just as she did.

"Mom to Shannon…Mom to Shannon. Come in, Shannon!"

She smiled and turned to her mom. "Right here. What do you need?" She glanced at the serving dishes in front of her, ready to pass any of them down the table.

"What I need is what we all need," she said, glancing around the full table, "and that is for you to join us next week at that Delaney gala. We'd like to see you get out of the house. To be with people. And we included you when we bought a table for eight. Have you thought about it a little more?"

How odd, the quiet that settled over the room. Even the little ones had stopped their chatter.

Despite her mother's attempt, Shannon was too old to be manipulated. "And you think ganging up on me at the dinner table is the way to go?" She shook her head. "Take your foot off the gas and put your good intentions elsewhere. I'll rejoin society when I'm ready."

"And when will that be?" asked her dad, who knew how to run a business and thought he could run a family. "Matthew's gone more than three years. You're young, Shannon, and vibrant, with a long life ahead. Is waiting five years the magic number? Six? The longer you hide out, the easier it is to keep hiding. It becomes a habit."

Her parents really were ganging up on her, with a double play made more powerful by the echo of yesterday's conversation with Andy. "I'm meeting the public at the art gallery," she said. "In fact, I'm actually the best staffer to meet and greet customers. So you can all stop worrying about me. I'm not hiding."

Her sister, Amy, reached for her hand and squeezed. "I know what they say about good intentions, but we thought this gala would be perfect, since you would have us all with you." A sweet smile crossed her face. "You know—that safety in numbers thing."

Shannon's tension ebbed away. Her sister had been nothing but loyal, helpful and loving since Shannon had returned to Boston permanently over a year ago. She pressed Amy's hand, but glanced around the table until her gaze rested on her grandfather.

"No opinion, Pops? Or is discretion the better part of valor for you?" Which would have been a first for the extrovert.

Her cherished Pops's brow furrowed, and his eyes narrowed as he took in the scene before him. "Don't listen to any of 'em. My money's on you to do what you think best."

She rose and walked over to the old man, leaned down and kissed him. "I love you, Pops."

"I love you, too. And if you decide to go, you can be my date!"

EXCERPT FROM
THE BROKEN CIRCLE
(NO ORDINARY FAMILY SERIES BOOK FIVE)

January 1995
Boston

A knock at her grad school apartment door pulled Lisa Delaney away from Commonwealth of Massachusetts vs. Torcelli Construction. Eyes burning, she rubbed her lids while, from her iPod, she heard Bryan Adams insist that everything he did, he did for her. Old song. Easy words. If the man really wanted to impress, he could take her contracts exam in the morning.

She pushed away from her desk, covered in law books and case briefs, and rose from her chair, stretching, bending and groaning. Her knees creaked like an arthritic old lady's. Shaking her head, she emitted a long sigh and promised herself a gym visit the next day—after the exam.

A second knock echoed, this time more impatiently

"I'm coming. Hang on." Nimble again, she rushed across the room and opened the door.

Her eyes widened, her stomach began to roil as she looked at two uniformed state troopers, snow melting on their jackets, cop faces in place. Her thoughts raced with possibilities. Classmates? Mike? Oh, please, not Mike.

"Are you Lisa Delaney?"

She stared at bad news and froze. All of her. Nothing worked. Not her mind, tongue, or breath. Perhaps her heart had stopped, too. One man coughed. The other repeated the question.

"I-I'm Lisa."

"Are your parents' names Robert and Grace Delaney?"

Oh, God, yes! Her heart raced at Mach speed, but she couldn't feel her legs at all. "What happened?"

"May we come in, Ms. Delaney?" Taller cop.

She nodded and pulled the door wider, but the knob slipped through her sweaty hands and she lost her balance.

"You might want to sit down."

As though moving underwater, she struggled into the closest chair.

"I'm afraid there's been an accident on the turnpike," began the quiet-till-now officer. "A fatal accident."

"Not…not my…my parents?" She barely got the words out before the officers' sympathetic silence answered her question.

"But that's impossible! I just spoke to my dad…"

"When was that, ma'am?"

When? When? "I think…maybe…last…last night…." Her voice drifted. Daddy had been checking up on his eldest, his numero uno child, joking with her about an apple a day. Staying healthy. A convenient excuse to call. To keep in touch with the one who'd left home. She'd understood his M.O. a month after arriving at school. Sweet, loving man. A man with a phone.

"Wh-what…?" Her throat closed.

The cops seemed to understand her intent. "The official investigation is ongoing, but according to preliminary reports, the other driver lost control of his vehicle and did a one-eighty."

"Drunk? But…but it's the middle of the week." As if that fact could change things.

"The driver's blood alcohol was normal."

"Then what…? The road…?"

"Icy conditions contributed. The temperature drops at night, and your folks were approaching at just the wrong moment. There were no survivors. I'm very sorry."

She nodded. *No survivors? Mom and Dad?* She wanted to cover her ears.

The other officer looked at his notes and said, "The Woodhaven police are with your brothers and sisters."

Oh, God, the kids… She had to get back to Woodhaven!

Standing quickly, she was hit by a wave of nausea and fell back into her chair. She doubled over, hand on her stomach. The phone rang, startling her further. She stared at the instrument, half-buried by textbooks, reached forward, and slowly lifted the receiver. "Hello?" she whispered.

"Lisa! Lisa! The police are here. Mom and Dad were in an accident. You have to come home! Now! I'm scared."

Jennifer. Her social butterfly teenage sister whose life revolved around boyfriends, best friends, and having fun. Except, not tonight. In the background, she heard the cacophony of younger voices crying and talking at the same time. She heard little Emily's high-pitched wail. "When is Lisa coming?"

"Hang on, Jen." She took a breath and looked at the officers. "There are four of them. Emily's only seven. My twin brothers are nine. Jen's sixteen. I've got to get there—a hundred miles—and I don't own a car." She couldn't afford one and didn't need one in a city with mass transit.

The troopers nodded, and she spoke into the phone again.

"I'll be there soon, Jen. As soon as I can. Maybe William and Irene can stay with you meanwhile." Her fiancé's parents lived across the street.

"They're not home. They went to Miami to see Mike play. Didn't you watch the game yesterday?"

"Of course I watched, but I didn't know his folks flew down." Mike had subbed for the starting quarterback and played an entire quarter. It was only his first year, but now the Riders were in the play-offs.

"So, Jen, you need to be in charge now until I get there. You and the kids sit tight and wait for me." She glanced toward the window, where falling snow was reflected by the light of the streetlamps.

"It might take a little while," she added. "It's a big trip, and the roads are bad…" What was she saying? Her parents had just been killed on those roads. "Jen, honey, let me talk to one of the officers there."

Her hand shook as she gave the receiver to the state cop. "Ask if they told the kids the truth."

In seconds, he shook his head. "Not yet. They're getting a social worker in on it."

She raised her eyes to his. "Please tell them not to do or say anything until I get there. Okay?"

Perspiration trickled from every pore. She shivered and sweated until finally her stomach lurched. Running into the bathroom, she vomited until nothing remained. Then she brushed her teeth, packed her suitcase to the brim, and snapped it shut. The sound focused her, and she inhaled a deep breath. *Be strong, be strong...*

One of the troopers held the door open. Her gaze skimmed the small apartment. She'd been happy there and ecstatic at being accepted into the program. She glanced at her textbooks before locking on to her college graduation photo. Her parents stood on either side of her, their smiles wide.

"Oh-h... One second." Her own future was now uncertain. Dropping her suitcase, she darted to the wall, took down the picture, and tucked it under her arm. Their dreams and her dreams might have to wait awhile.

#

Michael Brennan needed three days to get home to Woodhaven and to Lisa. It seemed like three years.

He tossed his luggage in his parents' front hall, turned around, and headed directly across the street. The Delaneys lived in a two-story wood-framed house with a front porch similar to his and to all the other homes on Hawthorne Street. He'd grown up there, but Lisa and her family had moved in over four years ago in June, right after her high school graduation. He'd graduated from a neighboring high school that same year. Their paths hadn't crossed until the evening his mother baked a cake and insisted their family welcome the new neighbors. Moaning and groaning, he'd given in, and the Brennans had gone to visit the Delaneys.

When Lisa opened the door and walked outside, he'd almost tripped up the front steps. One glance and he couldn't speak. His brain froze, too, as if a lightning bolt had slammed him head to toe. Big violet eyes, long, dark wavy hair, and a killer smile. A friendly smile. *Who wouldn't have fallen in love with her?* But he'd been the lucky one, the lucky guy who'd relished every single day since Lisa Delaney had first appeared at that front door.

Now her sidewalk needed shoveling. The streets had been plowed since the storm a few days ago, the walkways, too, but snow had fallen again yesterday, and surfaces had turned icy. He flexed his shoulders and entered the house. He'd take care of the snow after he wrapped his arms around her…if he could find her.

The Delaney house was packed. He recognized Lisa's aunts and uncles from out of -town, and all the neighbors, of course. Lisa's closest friends, Sandy and Gail, were there, too. Either they'd stayed all day or had just come from work. He waved and searched for his mom.

"Where's Lisa?"

"I'm glad you're here, Michael," she said, giving him a quick kiss, "but don't expect too much from Lisa. She's overwhelmed as…as we all are." Irene Brennan gazed up at the ceiling, indicating the second floor. "She's got the kids with her. The funeral's tomorrow, and she wants time alone with them."

"Alone doesn't include me."

He took the stairs two at a time, sensing the glances, the sympathy of the visitors as he made his way up. He appreciated their support, but they didn't have to worry. Surely, he could handle whatever he found. Surely, he and Lisa could handle it together.

He paused in the hallway at the top of the stairs. Each of the four bedroom doors stood ajar, but he could hear nothing. He started to push the first door open when, from the end of the corridor, he heard Lisa singing quietly, "Too-ra Loo-ra Loo-ra, Too-ra loo-ra lie…"

Was she trying to put the kids to sleep at five o'clock in the afternoon? He slowed his pace and walked the last few steps before knocking softly and entering the master bedroom. Lisa sat on her parents' bed, leaning against the headboard, the twins dozing on either side of her, little Emily sleeping on her lap. Jennifer lay across the foot of the bed, also sound asleep. He took it all in and understood that day and night had no meaning to them.

"Lisa..." A whispered prayer.

Her red-rimmed eyes brightened, her arms opened, and he was there. Kissing her and gently shifting one little brother lower on the mattress. She began to cry, her tears mingling with his as he rained kisses, and his tension melted simply by holding her in his arms. Tears flowed as he continued to embrace her and grieve while remembering Grace and Robert Delaney.

They'd been wonderful neighbors, wonderful parents, and good friends with his folks. The Delaneys had worked so hard to finally become "owners" instead of "renters," and celebrated their move to Hawthorne Street each time they'd made a mortgage payment. Lisa had told him how her dad would brandish the check and twirl Grace around the kitchen every single month. With their growing family, it had taken them fifteen years to afford their own home.

"How long can you stay?" Lisa whispered.

"He can't," mumbled nine-year-old Andy, rousing slightly. "He has to go to the conference championship game. And maybe to the Super Bowl."

"But not yet," Mike said, rubbing the boy's head with affection, but focusing his gaze on Lisa. "I'll be here for the funeral tomorrow. You won't be alone. Then I'll be back in a week. One short week." Which might feel like an eternity to Lisa.

"I'm glad, but-but everything has changed," she said, pulling a tissue from the nearby box and blotting her face. "We need to rethink our plans."

"The basics haven't changed," he replied quickly. "I love you, Lisa Delaney. And don't you forget it."

Her eyes shone. She pressed his hand, her fingers narrow and delicate around his broader ones. "I love you, too, but-but…." She sighed and glanced at the assorted children. "I'm not sure what's going to happen next," she said quietly.

"I am," he said. "I'm going to kiss you again."

And he did. When she kissed him back, when she lingered and leaned against him, he almost collapsed with relief. She was *the one* for him. No matter what. Her needs, the kids' needs….

"We'll sort it out when the time comes," he said. "I'll support you in every way I can." The logistics would no doubt be complicated, but he had faith that he and Lisa could do anything as long as they did it together.

She offered a wan smile. "I know you'll do your best, but you have commitments to the team. You're so talented! We all know you're being groomed as a starting quarterback, maybe even next year. So I think, for both our sakes, I need to handle this-this family situation by myself."

No, she didn't, but her brave effort tore a corner of his heart. "I think you're right about my place in the team," he said slowly, "but that's in our favor. The money's good." He'd worked hard with his coaches, and his natural talents had been recognized. His dream career loomed just over the horizon.

"I must be weird," said Lisa. "I never think about your salary. Even your first year minimum is like make-believe Monopoly money to me. It doesn't matter. I'm just so…so proud of you."

Men cry. Even big football players. But once that afternoon was enough. His throat ached as he swallowed to stem more tears. Lisa needed him to be strong.

"Have I ever told you about my conversation with your dad at the end of the summer you moved to Hawthorne Street?" he asked. "It was right before I went off to Ohio State on my scholarship."

"All Daddy told me was that you were too big for your britches, but he was laughing."

A surge of love and a wave of sadness—both raced through Mike. The words sounded exactly like something Rob Delaney would say. And the laughter—well, laughter was the norm in Lisa's family. Her dad loved to tell a good story and could imitate the comedy greats and their jokes. Rob had been a natural "on stage," and no one had a bigger heart.

"Before I left for college," Mike continued, "I told him I was going to marry you someday."

"You've got to be kidding! We were only eighteen. We'd just met that very summer." For a moment, her expression lightened. She tipped her head back, and her eyes met his. "And what did he say?"

"He said that I'd better treat you like gold— always. And I promised I would."

"O-o-h…." Despair once again etched her face. "Our lives… everything..."—she waved her arm— "has changed. I can't-I *won't* hold you to any promise."

"You have no vote." He kissed her again, vowing to keep that promise. Loving Lisa was the easy part. Building a solid future together…well, that goal might be more difficult to reach now. Lisa was in no condition to make any decisions. Their next steps would be decided by him.

His gaze rested on each of the youngsters, one at a time. Four sweet, innocent children. Without warning, his heart started to race, and his palms became covered in sweat. Fear. Like Lisa, he was almost twenty-three, and deep down, he was scared, too. He had no experience with kids, not even a younger brother or sister. But he wouldn't give himself away, wouldn't let Lisa know. A quarterback led with confidence on the field. Now he had to do the same at home.

LINDA BARRETT BOOKS

NOVELS—ROMANCE

No Ordinary Family Series
Unforgettable (Bk. 1)

Safe at Home (Bk. 2)

Heartstrings (Bk. 3)

His Greatest Catch (Bk. 4)

The Broken Circle (Bk. 5)

Starting Over Series

True-Blue Texan (Bk 1)

A Man of Honor (Bk. 2)

Love, Money and Amanda Shaw (Bk.3)

The Inn at Oak Creek (Bk.4)

Flying Solo Series

Summer at the Lake (Bk. 1)

Houseful of Strangers (Bk. 2)

Quarterback Daddy (Bk. 3)

The Apple Orchard (Bk. 4)

Pilgrim Cove Series

The House on the Beach (Bk. 1)

No Ordinary Summer (Bk. 2)

Reluctant Housemates (Bk. 3)

The Daughter He Never Knew (Bk. 4)

Sea View House Series

Her Long Walk Home (Bk. 1)

Her Picture-Perfect Family (Bk. 2)

Her Second-Chance Hero (Bk. 3)

NOVELS—WOMEN'S FICTION

The Broken Circle

The Soldier and the Rose

Family Interrupted

For Better or Worse – A boxed set of all three WF novels at a discounted price

SHORT NOVELLA

Man of the House

MEMOIR

HOPEFULLY EVER AFTER: Breast Cancer, Life and Me (true story about surviving breast cancer twice)

Printed in Great Britain
by Amazon

49117666R00109